Cocktales

3 eras, 3 tales, 3 bars

by

Chantz Perkins

House of Cheng

The Gold Ring

Tattooed Chica

LGBTQ+ novelettes collection

Cocktales

Copyright © 2024 by Chantz Perkins

All rights reserved.

No part of this publication may be reproduced, distributed, or transmitted in any form or by any means, including photocopying, recording, or other electronic or mechanical methods, without the prior written permission of the publisher, except as permitted by U.S. copyright law. For permission requests, contact http://artbychantz.com

The story, all names, characters, and incidents portrayed in this production are fictitious. No identification with actual persons (living or deceased), places, buildings, and products is intended or should be inferred.

First edition published by AnyBookPress, via American Book Center, Amsterdam, the Netherlands, for author Chantz Perkins, also known as R.G. Perkins, on 4/24

2nd edition published by artbychantz press for Chantz Perkins, aka R.G. Perkins, on 5/24.

Chantz Perkins aka R.G.Perkins asserts the moral right to be identified as the author of this work in accordance with Dutch Copyright Law, Autheurwet and the USA Copyright law.

Text and images are copyrighted by Chantz Perkins and artbychantz, all rights reserved.

Cover design by artbychantz.

This collection is dedicated to the many generations who fought for equality and equal rights.

Move forward, not back.

The three novelettes in this collection are reproduced by AnyBookPress, Amsterdam and artbychantz publishers.

Copyright by Chantz Perkins

House of Cheng   2023

The Gold Ring   2023

Tattooed Chica   2023

Forward

In writing the three stories of my book, *Cocktales,* I explore the conversations and concerns of my gay characters. Each story begins in a gay bar. The reason for this is because of my own life experience. As a child of the sixties, I didn't come out until the eighties, which was when I discovered gay bars. I found them to be a safe place to socialize, share political views, and discuss gay rights.

Not so many gay bars around anymore, but their effect on our generation and culture was already inspirational. Meeting together made us stronger and provided the unity we needed to fight back against homophobia. The stories I wrote come directly from those days when I was observing my place in society. My sense of belonging to a club where words like "lezzie" and "queer" were hurled at us in mockery and derision notwithstanding.

Now, I wield those same words proudly to describe myself and my culture. I found a way to convey my own experience without apologies or excuses. I'm a proud lesbian and my stories are my gift, and an insight to a community that is very inclusive and compassionate. I offer the reader a glimpse of my lifestyle and observations. My intention is to educate and enlighten.

Most of all, my purpose for writing these novelettes are to provide my own perspective on how some people manage to thrive in this world, not just survive.

CONTENTS

HOUSE OF CHENG

page 9

THE GOLD RING

page 83

TATTOOED CHICA

page 145

This novelette is dedicated to all the women whose lack of choice endangered both their lives and livelihood.

.

House Of Cheng

by Chantz Perkins

HOUSE OF CHENG

By

CHANTZ PERKINS

House of Cheng

The Street
Page
The Dragon Lady
The Ping Ting Room
Roy
At the Bar
Kay
The Meeting

The Street

The asphalt street glistens, a tsunami wave sliding through the city like a snake. From downtown past tinseltown into Hollywood, women dressed in short skirts and low tops lean into open car windows, their red lips bargaining in strict "cash only" terms. Slithering beneath the yet unrisen rainbows into West Hollywood, pink melts into streams of nomadic sex, past billboards looming over rock clubs, where inside cocktails swap for hotel room keys. Jetting toward Beverly Hills, pillars stand erect in old wealth tradition.

Toward ancient cinemas of Westwood, films tell stories that the famed university dared not. Zipping into Bel Air, left right left along Deadman's Curve, over smoking leather jackets, crumpled Chevy hot rods gasp a last breath, on the day the music died. Gliding into the green of Brentwood, buses of tourists click homes of long dead stars, as Marilyn rests naked, finally in peace.

Behind the squat, one-story high buildings: an office building, a stationer and a bank. Between sits a structure devoid of windows.

The street is named Sunset Boulevard. In front of the windowless structure, Page Dubois now stands, irresolute. Huge, black doors loom before her. Each can be opened by pulling on one or the other large brass ring. And although she's stood here hundreds of times in the last twenty years, tonight, the doors seem suddenly forbidden. With one hand on the brass ring, Page wavers, wondering how she came to be here tonight.

Page

Even by city standards, the heat of the day had been grueling. Page began her morning at 7 a.m., sweltering with no air conditioning in her Studebaker Wagonaire. Cars screeched past as her station wagon coughed and wheezed along the freeway, sun screaming through the windshield onto the cracked dashboard and between her breasts.

Her first appointment had been to a housing tract property over the mountains into the San Fernando Valley: a place where no breeze stirred from the beach to scatter the brown smog trapped inside its belly but instead, created a cesspool of heat suffocating her like a sauna. Standing inside the hellhole, she thought, *How anyone can live here, I'll never understand.*

Her client, fresh from New York, had not understood the cesspool either. "Christ!" he exclaimed, wiping sweat with a handkerchief from the back of his neck, "Is it always this hot?" Then he told her "I'll have to think the property over, preferably poolside under an umbrella with a cold drink. Care to join me?" he asked expectantly.

"Mmmm," Page hesitated, "My calendar is filled with appointments all day so…"

The client drifted back to his car, tie loosened, jacket thrown over his shoulder, as great pools formed in his armpits. Page concluded from his pout there would be no sale today, if ever.

Driving the back route from the valley along the Cahuenga Pass into the Hollywood Hills, she pulled her car off the narrow winding street, into the carport. She looked the place over, attempting to see, if any, best features. The house had affectionately been named, "The Chalet" by her male colleagues. *The joke is obviously on me,* she thought, realizing with a jolt that she'd been given scraps from the bottom of the barrel.

The house, painted a dirty chocolate color, its surface peeling, looked as weary as the willows that wept further down the canyon.

Her client tooted the horn as he drove up in a shiny, new Corvette convertible Stingray, pulling next to her ancient station wagon. *Like beauty and the beast,* she thought, viewing the cars side by side.

Page greeted the man of forty, stylishly dressed in a pale blue blazer with a silk scarf tied at his neck.

Leading him inside "The Chalet," they paused at what she'd decided was the best feature: a stunning view of the city that stretched out before them. Upon closer inspection, Page thought, *a windswept day would have better suited this showing.* The heat of the day had marred the beauty. Honey brown smog floated over the city like a bubbling stew.

Page, her face now crimson from embarrassment as well as the heat, led him through the rickety structure. It balanced on two toothpicks of rotting wood: a house of cards that the next strong wind could easily snap off the hillside and send crashing below. Her client had not even pretended to be interested in the house. He was more entranced with her than the tired, old chalet.

Page's final showing had been through rush hour traffic, above the tiny suburb she called home. There, a horrid, little man had attempted to bargain down the price as he ogled her breasts. Page knew he would not buy. It was clear as crystal that his wife held the purse strings as tightly as a Titanic passenger clinging to her life raft.

Finally home, Page nibbled at the remains of her dinner, chewing over her lousy day. Traditional pot roast and potatoes had transformed into TV dinners the moment the ink of her signature on the divorce papers had dried. *After our kids were born,* she thought, remembering her husband of twenty years. He'd slid from art studies into law, taking up the new role of suit and tie corporate lawyer as valiantly as he'd earlier grasped a paintbrush.

"Just another challenge," he'd said, "I never saw myself as a great painter anyway. The only way artists make money is after they die."

That line had closed the door on his artist life, bolting it shut behind him. Page shook her head and tried again to recall when exactly the ripple of caution inside her became a red flag of suspicion.

She'd met his secretary only once. A surprisingly young girl, bright-eyed with glossy, blonde hair.

Page's lifelong trust of him and their long years of commitment had never wavered. The shock of his affair had cut her deeply.

Only the regular routine of raising three kids sutured the hole in her heart. Instead of quarrels, demands, and threats, she'd bitten her lip and kept their home beautiful, waiting with an open heart for his return.

Her fantasy of reconciled bliss never came. Instead, he'd demanded a divorce while avoiding her eyes. She thought, *The picket fence happy ending I'd been promised in marriage ended instead like a car crash.*

She perched in front of her oval mirror, blinking at her reflection. Not a sound stirred in the apartment: no knock on the door as the kids fought for turns in the morning, no shouts of "Hurry up!" No cries of "Bye, Mom!" as they ran out the door. *Yep,* Page thought to herself, *it's been a long twenty years.*

Her three kids, one girl and two boys, all of them almost in high school now, had escaped to wherever teenagers go on a Friday night. Where exactly that was, she really didn't want to know.

Lines and pouches snickered beneath her eyes. She applied cream to her face, then powder and blush. Listening, she sighed, *Our home is so quiet now. Soon, every night will be this way, looking at a stranger's face in the mirror surrounded by silence.*

"Stop it!" she scolded herself, snatching the pale blue eye shadow to accent her slate gray eyes, adding a thick line of deep blue liner and spiky fake lashes.

She sang aloud her favorite line from the current Broadway musical, *South Pacific*, "I'm gonna wash that man right outta my hair," to lighten her mood.

Brushing her glossy brown hair up and off her shoulders, she swept it under her neck like a sea wave, curling it into an inside flip. Noting that her shoulders had tanned from the day's sun she said, "Well, fine. In place of my commission on a home sale, I have brown shoulders. Fair enough."

Spraying immense clouds of Aquanet to freeze her hairdo, she mumbled a silent prayer to the angels of hair, "Please hold until next week's appointment."

Finally, a bohemian touch of round, red plastic earrings clipped on her petite lobes, their hue perfectly matching her tight, sleeveless dress. With a dab of fragrance and a slash of red to her lips, she slipped into black heels. Snatching a light cardigan, clutch purse, and with her keys in hand, she left through the door.

Kids will be home sometime, she thought as she tapped up the street. *Out doing who knows what tonight? God, please not getting pregnant or impregnating some girl.* Page quickened her pace to escape the thought.

Their modest apartment, rented after her husband sold their home, was the sole survivor of the post World War II building boom. *Neglected and worn out,* she fretted, *compared with these beautiful homes lining the street.*

Again, she relished every house, their classic wood frames, painted in identical shades of pale yellow with darker trim. A small emerald lawn in front, trimmed in violet pansies, red roses, or daisies, gave each one a loved and well cared for warmth.

Page strode up the street, her head raised to see the hills emerge as a Chinese screen landscape: translucent blue patterns overlapping as they receded, each one a mere memory of the one before it, the farthest echoing the fading sky. At night, the hills merged into one huge Goliath mass rising over the tiny town. To embrace or to crush it? Page was never quite sure.

Page walked past golden medallion trees, fallen blossoms painted the street a carpet of vibrant yellow. She tapped briskly up the street toward the center of town, her journey ending at the favorite watering hole of every unwed over twenty-one-year-old in town.

Page stood, perched in heels, her dress snug as skin, sleeveless, arms chilling in the cool night air. Her earrings gleamed in the light of a passing car. She turned from the glare towards the doors and thought, *I've come here hundreds of times in twenty years.* But tonight, alone and unchaperoned, she hesitated.

The massive doors loomed before her as a huge, dark force; an immense genie with bulging arms across his chest, and on his wrists, large brass rings. The doors could be opened by pulling one or the other ring but as she stood before them, the rings looked to her like eyes; large, round and surprised to see her.

Taking a deep breath, Page plucked up her nerve. Timidly as a spooked cat, she opened the door. Mrs. Cheng, the owner, also known as "the Dragon Lady," politely greeted Page with a small bow. Her ivory face, high cheek-boned and heart-shaped, contrasted pale green eye shadow and a wing of emerald eye liner. Jet black hair, tightly pulled into a bun with a streak of silver through the brow line, completed the look. Mrs. Cheng's red lips curled so delicately, Page thought she'd imagined their smile. Speaking softly in formal English with roots of her Chinese ancestry, she said, "Table for…" as her jade eyes swept discreetly past Page into the empty street, "one?"

    Page blushed and stepped through the door. Cool, dim lights of the Orient greeted her. A warm rush of hot cooking oil and aromas of marinated pork rose deliciously into her nose. Surrounding her stood rows of perfectly aligned, square, black lacquered tables, each with four high-backed, ebony chairs tucked neatly beneath a crisp, pink linen tablecloth. Perched on each table was a small Chinese lantern, where inside, a small flame glowed.

    Page listened to the muffled shifting of cutlery, the gathering of plates by silent waiters, the quiet murmur of voices blending with enthusiastic munching of egg rolls, smacking of sticky spareribs, and the clicking of chopsticks. Each meal ended with almond cookies alongside the favored fortune cookies. Many a conflict arose from the words nestled inside these cookies. Page listened to a nearby table as a squabble began to brew.

"Here, honey, you open mine," said by a mother to her six-year-old son.

The boy cracked open the cookie and read, "'Good fortune rewards those who strive for it.'"

His mother replied, "Very good, Joey," then turned to his father and said, "There, you see? You need to ask for that raise or quit your job…"

"Huh?" he answered, "Where does it say that?"

"Right here," she stabbed at the words, "'To those who strive for it' Strive… it's right here."

The father answered. "That's just a Chinese trick, it's not real… it can't be." The boy rolled his eyes and munched his cookie.

That could have been me ten years ago, Page thought suddenly as images of her kids and husband materialized before her. Shifting her eyes from the memory, she replied, "No table just now… maybe later."

Mrs. Cheng nodded and moved toward the bar. With scarlet-nailed fingers, she parted and held open an ebony curtain of hanging beads.

Page remembered rumors about Mrs. Cheng, who had been stamped as "The Dragon Lady," a name never said to her face, and its inception remained unclear.

Gossip told the story that Mrs. Cheng and her husband, a short, round-bellied, little man who never stayed past 8 p.m., had been involved in a crisis of some sort, and the name had something to do with it.

The restaurant seemed to hang on shakily for a few years until Mrs. Cheng had stepped in, taking control of him, the staff and the restaurant, and transforming it into the best, and only Chinese restaurant in town.

She then hired Sammy as bartender, veering its bar, *The Ping Ting Room,* into the most popular place in town. The Chengs had become not only prosperous, but downright rich.

Page hadn't really understood why Mrs. Cheng had been code-named "The Dragon Lady," but it suited her, right down to the tight, mint green, cheongsam Suzie Wong dress she wore and tiny black pumps.

The rumor went on to tell that Mrs. Cheng had somehow become the owner and now, she, a woman in 1970, was the sole admiral of this very profitable ship.

Whether feared or respected, Mrs. Cheng had the face of a China doll, albeit an older one, who never gave away a thing. Her piercing, jade green eyes held within them the fire of a dragon.

Page nodded to her and timidly stepped into the bar. Cigarette smoke rose in plumes toward the ceiling where tasseled red paper lanterns hung with points in gold. Page blinked into the dim light, moving cautiously forward.

The space was dark, intimate, and tonight, dangerous. As she inched towards the silhouettes, "The Dragon Lady" let the curtain fall, its snapping sound of beads shutting behind her, closing her in.

The Dragon Lady

Mrs. Cheng roamed through the restaurant, nodding and smiling to her customers. Stopping abruptly at a tray of dirty dishes stacked on the back table, she turned to one of her waiters and fiercely whispered in Chinese, "Get this out of here! What am I paying you for? To smoke in the alley!?"

The waiter hurried to pick up the tray mumbling apologies in Chinese but under his breath in English, he murmured, "Lezzie."

Her jade eyes sliced his retreating silhouette but then she let it go. "I'll fire him, next week, maybe," she grumbled. "For now, I can't risk anymore gossip."

She thought, *'Lezzie' I've not heard that word for a long time. Not since I was sixteen.*

She recalled those years with a mixture of anger and affection. Then, she was a young girl named June with beauty so rare, people thought her to be twenty. *Watching my idols on the silver screen,* she remembered with glee. *Ditching school and handing my lunch money of four quarters to the cashier at the downtown movie palace.*

Walking through the foyer, she'd pause to gaze toward the poster of her icon, Rita Hayworth, bold letters spelling out the title, *Gilda!* slashed diagonally across the top.

Rita stood shapely nonchalant, a long, flowing gown clinging to her hips. Brown hair cascading, her head cocked indifferently to one side, smirking at the men surrounding her, as smoke curled from the cigarette at her fingertips.

June sighed as she strolled into the lobby. A plush carpet rolled toward her, wave patterned in burgundy, as marble columns stood attention on the perimeter. Before her swept a grand staircase. *Plucked straight from a movie,* she smiled to herself as she climbed the stairs.

The cheap seats, located in the far reaches of the third balcony, were an effort to climb but she knew they were worth every step. From the last seat, a sweeping grandeur of the whole theater could be seen.

A young usher stepped forward and reached for her ticket. He was smartly dressed in a sharp red uniform with brass-buttoned jacket, pants striped black along the leg and a box cap with a chin strap. *She's really pretty,* he thought, noticing her strange green eyes. He couldn't pull his away.

With a crackling voice, he asked her, "Want me to help ya find yer seat?" eagerly gazing at her.

June replied curtly with a firm, "No," walking past him.

Stunned, he pointed to the third balcony stairs, inwardly grumbling, *I should never bother with folks in the cheap seats. Hell, I never go all the way up there at all, not unless I want to sneak a smoke, or get a complaint,* he chuckled, *then my flashlight beam hits their faces like a deer in the headlights, catching them, doing their funny stuff, stuff I don't wanna know about.*

As she climbed the stairs, he watched her with a smirk and thought, *She is really pretty though, almost like a star with those strange green eyes. But she answered me kinda snooty-like. She's kinda stuck up… for a Chinese.*

June edged through the row, choosing the furthest seat in the back. Settling into the plush, red velvet seat, she gazed up at the chandeliers. Patterns of triangles within smaller triangles reflected on the deep blue ceiling. To her right hung a curtain hiding a grand organ. No longer needed, it had once accompanied vaudeville acts where men danced like monkeys and women chirped like parrots.

Hundreds of seats spread out before her towards the stage. Beneath was the orchestra pit, where previously, a live orchestra accompanied the silent films.

The house lights dimmed. June settled back, a jolt of expectation buzzing through her. As the red velour curtain slowly opened, her eyes widened with anticipation.

Comical stunts danced across the screen: helmeted cops in police cars chased goofy criminals, men dangled from high-rise buildings, race cars toppled and crashed. Then the news reels began. Horrors of the war that just ended in Europe threw shock waves through the audience.

June turned away from the gruesome pictures toward the silhouettes surrounding her. In the screen flashes, she caught sight of old men eagerly submitting to younger men's affections, while women stole kisses from each other behind the cover of a *Star* magazine. This was not the first time she'd viewed these off-screen fantasies. She'd been shocked at first, then oddly intrigued.

June wanted to love a woman in ways she dared not. In the dark, in secret, behind closed doors. The dark felt seductive, dangerous, a place she wanted very much to be. A territory foreign to her culture and upbringing. The shabby downtown apartment she shared with her parents: four flights up from the dirty alleys and its stinking garbage. Seeing the faces of the people who spoke languages she did not understand. *We do share a bond though,* she thought, *we're poor and seen by white people as foreigners, not Americans.*

She thought, *On the screen, men in crisp tuxedoes dance with women in clinging gowns, champagne flowing. A world I may never afford. Yet around me, in the cheap seats, sit the poor. Taking their one chance to be together, stealing moments with lovers in the dark.* Two opposite worlds, here, within her reach. June sat in her velvet seat, determined to have both.

Actions toward these goals soon followed. A friend who worked at the studios told her about an opening for a role in a movie currently in production. June had sprung to the challenge by ditching school, arriving promptly at 7 a.m. The line of hopeful actors was long, but June's jade eyes caught the attention of the casting agent, landing her an uncredited role as an extra. Several nonspeaking roles later, the management had swept her into a six-month contract, their expertise somehow avoiding her dad's signature or her age as an issue.

Mrs. Cheng folded the napkins, remembering the excitement of that time when her moment of fame had finally arrived: *A Chinese lead speaking role!* she grinned with pride, *I received good reviews too! "The Butterfly" they'd named me, but also, "The Dragon Lady,"* she grumbled. *But they couldn't deny the acclaim I'd received from the public.* Then she stopped, remembering, *But the studio owners had no backbone. They'd made me into a star, then didn't know what to do with me. They'd told me, "You're a fine actress but we don't see you as a lead." The truth was the studio caved in and had succumbed to the prejudice then. Chinese roles were given to Hungarians, Germans, anyone except a Chinese!*

Why is it that men in power are all cowards!?

Mr. Cheng sat in the backroom. She paused, then bent over him, and loosened his tie. "Come now, silly," she cooed affectionately, "you will choke."

He looked up at her and scolded, "Like you care!"

She stiffened, looking at him, then softened, remembering their beginning, the two of them newly married. *It had been after her father had found out about her time at the studios. Then the battle began,* she remembered, *when Dad found out how I was spending my time... and with whom.*

The fashionable semi-stars had taken June under their collective wing, showing more of Hollywood to her than she'd ever imagined.

And boy! Did Dad get angry! She remembered him shouting, *"Think of your mother! You're killing her! Look! Her heart is breaking!"* June had sheepishly looked at her mother's shrunken body and knew it was true. Guilt washed over her.

Too young to move out and with little income, June's willful streak had ended abruptly in an arranged marriage to her father's colleague. *An older man of course,* she thought scornfully, then softened, *but Mr. Cheng never caused me trouble, never yelled, or hit me. He was always quiet. He'd only had praise for me then,* she recalled, *during our courtship. But he'd probably heard the rumors about me though Dad tried his best to stifle them, word had gotten around. That was so long ago,* she sighed, *before his own dad died and he inherited this place.* She thought, *after you got the restaurant, I thought, finally! No more cheap, ugly downtown apartment.* She remembered the area with her nose. It stank.

June's mind flashed on those she'd lived alongside then. *A ragtag mix of immigrants. Chinese, of course, but also Japanese, Irish, German, Polish, and Italians. Our bond was that few of us spoke English, and all were hated by the white-faced Americans.* "Foreigners!" *they grumbled,* "weird customs, strange food."

Still, she thought, *that small corner of the city was like our own tiny village: Filled with good hearted people... and so entertaining! The Irish who loved their whisky! And those Italians and their vino!*

June recalled the faces with affection as she'd watched them: *strolling with kids to MacArthur Park, sitting on the grass eating homemade food brimming from picnic baskets, drinking bottles of wine, looking out at the water... like they were in Venice or something! It was beautiful there,* closing her eyes, she saw colorful lights shimmering on the water, small boats with lovers, an evening breeze cooling the stifling night air. *Magical times...*

Her eyes softened as she looked at her husband and said, "But I do care, you know I do. I care for you as the twilight breeze tickles the stream," tickling him under his chin, bringing a sparkle into his eyes. He giggled, his round Buddha belly jiggling up and down.

"There now, you see?" she said, "I'm not such… a dragon." The name had almost become a joke between them.

It occurred after she took over as manager when the rumors began that she'd first heard "Dragon Lady" hissed behind her back. The words stung like a scorpion.

"Oh, June," Mr. Cheng had said, "these white folks don't mean anything by it. It's just their ignorance, the way they were brought up… or maybe just too much alcohol."

"Then why didn't they name me 'Butterfly?!'" she'd snapped back crossly.

It had been after the rumors began that Mr. Cheng turned away from his beautiful yet oddly unobtainable wife, toward demons of his own.

Mrs. Cheng folded the pink linen and thought, *Yet his kind words flowed over me like a summer rain, cleansing my fury,* then she recalled, *that was an awful time for us. First, my suspicions, then finally, his confession. Damn, I should have known he wasn't at his cousin's place in San Francisco but out feeding his addiction. Why had he lied to me?* She knew of course. Their marriage had been a caring but expressionless affair.

"Now his scorn echoes my father's," she said aloud.

"What did you say?" her husband asked.

"Oh, nothing," she replied, "Isn't it 8 o'clock?" He rose from his chair. She pecked him on the cheek.

He said, "I'll see you later" as he closed the door.

Mrs. Cheng looked around the back room, tidy because of her efforts. She recalled what came next: her husband's confession.

It began innocently enough, she remembered, *playing Mahjong with his friends on Sundays. Then came horse racing at Hollywood Park.* "Damn!" she cursed. *I should have known he wasn't spending the weekend at his cousin's place in San Francisco but out feeding his addiction… in Reno of all places!*

Then a huge loss at the roulette wheel. Shame-faced, he'd handed the restaurant ownership papers over, as payment. She thought, *with one spin of that damned silver ball, we almost lost everything.*

June had always been a straightforward thinker. Problems for her had only been a puzzle that needed clear thinking to solve. She remembered the cowards who'd manipulated her all her life. *NO!* she thought, *I will not let that happen to me... not anymore!*

Just when it seemed nothing would ever go right, three things occurred simultaneously to change our lives completely. The first... we finally got a permit to sell alcohol. In a small town like this, families, couples, and singles love their alcohol. With only two other bars in town, one a tough bar for servicemen, now ironically a gay bar, or had it always been? Probably. And the other one too far up the coast. Ours was the one they walked to. Yes, she thought, *the alcohol license was a huge victory. Then I stole Sammy to bartend from that Tiki bar in midtown. His dry wit and strong drinks secured a loyal and thirsty clientele.*

June smiled at the next steps she put into place to pay the debt. Using her beauty and the sophistication she'd learned in Hollywood; she charmed the casino owners into renegotiating the debt. *I told them, "What do you want with a decrepit old Chinese restaurant? Isn't cash more your style? If you let me keep the papers, I can get a bank loan to pay you back - with interest. Without the papers... well..."* June let the sentence dangle while they agreed to her way of thinking.

She had obsessively kept the news of the alcohol permit secret from the casino owners. *When they eventually learned the facts, instead of anger,* she grinned, *they'd laughed! I too had a streak of bluff about me, and they*

36

respected it. They acknowledged her shrewd tactics by buying her a drink, then becoming her best customers.

June innocently told the bank manager next door, "We need improvements. Good fortune has rewarded our hard work! We've obtained a permit to sell alcohol! Think of the business!" The manager thought instead of the interest rate, readily agreeing to a loan, signed by her husband, of course.

The loan secured and debt on the way out, she'd told her husband, "Your disease can be cured, but only with professional help." She'd learned of a Gamblers Anonymous in San Francisco, where his cousin, who'd already drawn her scorn from the Reno fiasco, swore to accompany him to the meetings and keep an eye on him. She sent Mr. Cheng there for two years. *But not before,* she smiled now, *first convincing him to sign the ownership papers over to me… "Just for safety's sake,"* she'd told him.

The Ping Ting Room

Page leaned against the cigarette machine by the entrance, watching the crowds, the excitement buzzing around her. Dotting the circumference of the room were small, half-moon, black leather booths, sitting four or squeezing five. Crowds of boisterous men and women with drinks in hand sat or stood three deep at the bar. All shapes of glasses: short, stout, and thick for scotch and soda, or thin- stemmed, funneled for martinis, garnished with plump, mint green olives and red pimento stuffed inside.

The groups smoked and laughed, chortled, and shouted, explosions of laughter from each cluster as the night ticked forward. Each man or woman tried their best to look sober without seeming eager, consuming as many drinks as possible before the bar closed at 2 a.m.

The women, divorced and happy, out for the first time without a husband in years, tried to relish their newfound freedom. Smiles painted on faces, "old college try" charm attempting to be found anew as fear and excitement of new, single womanhood fizzed inside every one of them.

The men, married and unhappy, stood in short-sleeved, white shirts with a pocket over the breast, their skinny black ties loosened. Most worked in the aerospace industry and had come straight from work.

Each and every one of them had used the payphone in the back, dialed their respective wives, spoke into the receiver the same line: "Honey, I have to work late tonight."

A woman dressed in a bright, colorful, sleeveless dress, rose from the bar, her destination: the ladies room. A strategic choice of route was needed; either through the front black beaded curtains, past "The Dragon Lady," through the restaurant, and one never knew who one may see there, neighbors with kids or ex-lovers. Or the back way, squeezing past crowds at the bar, toward the rear, through the other beaded curtains, then to the left.

Her route chosen, a quick pee and lopsided lipstick replaced, she walked back to the bar, fingers crossed that her companion had not left in search of another woman. She slid atop her stool to see. *Yes, he's gone.*

Sammy the bartender polished a glass with a bar towel and looked into her tired, hazel eyes. He smiled, then motioned toward the front entrance, silently telling her, *He's only gone for a pack of smokes*, as his friendly brown eyes slid discreetly toward the cigarette machine. Her brow eased as she smiled at Sammy in gratitude: The secret safe between them.

Page leaned against the cigarette machine, head bowed to focus on the deep blue carpet. She thought, *Thin and a bit worn, but who can see stains in this low light?*

With uneasy envy, she looked toward a bright-eyed woman with soprano laughter. Wrapped in the cloak of fun while within, she glowed. *There's one like her, at every party, everywhere,* she thought, *even in my days at the university, I mingled and smiled, but I never had that sort of spark.*

The cigarette machine flexed its muscles, proudly viewing the packs on display: Marlboro, Winston, Parliament and Camel, or Salem, Newport, and Kool for a dollar a pack.

A man reached toward the machine and dropped coins in, "clink, ca-clunk," signaling success. Reaching to the button, he chose the brand, then pulled the knob toward him, and bent down. His fist eagerly gripped a pack of Camels from inside the flap door.

He leaned nonchalantly against the machine, his eyes never leaving her face. Very slowly, he unwrapped the cellophane cover, opened the pack and put a cigarette to his lips, lighting it with a silver Zippo lighter.

In the flame's glow, Page watched a hard face of dubious integrity. *There is something suave about him though,* she thought to herself, *despite his unwashed blonde hair.* As one lock fell into his steel blue eyes she thought, *He's either just awoken and slightly sexy, or lazy and out of work.* For her, this remained for now, undetermined.

He flipped the top of his Zippo shut with a quick snap, closing out the flame. Then with a jolt, he said, "Oh! I'm sorry, would you like one?" as he held the pack toward her.

"No - no thank you," she said, as her eyes ran away from his face, "I'd just like a drink at the moment, but," Page could see no free space to sit anywhere.

"Here, let me," he said, "I'll find you a seat at the bar, next to me."

Roy

Had he had lived in Hollywood, his name could have been Dakota. But since he lived in the suburbs, he was just called Roy.

His long, blonde hair hung over his shoulders, which he purposely kept unwashed so babes would think he surfed. His blue eyes looked clear when lighthearted, but would flash anger when crossed, which was often.

He had few friends because many had become fed up with his antics. However, his looks could easily attract the most attractive women, so this kept him popular, though most men thought him kind of a jerk.

Mmmmm, Roy thought as his blue eye s scanned the bar, *this night is lookin' good numero uno,* then mused, *nope. Can't go back to where I was sitting... but hey! Far out!* Roy saw his friend, Johnnie sitting at the bar. *He'll make room for her.*

"Damn! Why's it always so packed in here?" he grumbled," not even with chicks, but dudes! What's up with that?"

Still, he thought, *I always score 9 outta 10 and tonight don't look no different. Gotta try out my bitchin' new waterbed... Mmmm yes! Lookin' to put a few more notches in my belt tonight. She's foxy too. Kinda old, probably divorced... but who cares? Not me!* Smiling wickedly, he remembered *I've got a full pack of smokes, cash... Hmmm.* He fretted, *How much have I spent? Oh, well, no problemo. I'll just hit up Johnnie if I'm low. This won't take no time at all.*

Shit! I gotta work early tomorrow. Well, fuck 'em. They can stick it where the sun don't shine. They're all stuck-up chumps anyway... lookin' down on me. So what if I flunked outta high school? That wasn't my fault... it was Dad's. He's been a pain in my ass since Mom died.

Roy pictured her face in front of him. *You didn't deserve it, Mom,* he thought. Then his father's face appeared like the devil. *Bastard! Wouldn't even give me cash for city college, to get a degree in engineerin'. I coulda done it too, if he'd only let go of his damn bottle long enough to put his hand in his pocket, the stingy bastard. But noooo... he'd rocked in that ratty, old rocking chair sayin' "I'm a man!"*

I told him, "I'm a man too." The chair stopped rocking. Then Dad's eyes locked on mine.

He said, "You? A man?"

Then he laughed that hysterical laugh I hate and said, "You didn't even enlist when the President went into Vietnam against the commies. No! You ran away to Canada. And NO!

I won't lie to the cops for you. So just make me a drink or get outta my face, you pansy."

Roy had said nothing. Red-faced, he walked into his room and packed, leaving all traces of his boyhood behind, except one: an old, cracked, black and white photograph of his mother. Her face appeared before him now like an angel. He thought, *Damn, I miss you. You deserved better, Mom. Why the hell didn't ya leave him?*

Suddenly, a man bumped into him. Roy quickly swiped a tear from his eye and shouted, "Hey!"

The man replied, "Wow... mellow out, man... everything's cool. Peace," as he held up two fingers in a peace sign.

Roy replied, "Yeah, whatever... peace to you too," then he flashed his middle finger.

The man said, "Take a chill pill, man... you're trippin'" as he moved away.

Roy thought, *Okay, Roy, don't sweat it... just forget this jerk and call in sick tomorrow. Yeah! That chick in reception might even feel sorry for me and bring me a pot roast or somethin'... Even stay the night. Yeah,* he thought, *gonna take care of business and break in that waterbed. If not this brunette, then maybe the receptionist...*

At the Bar

Roy nudged his buddy at the bar. He rose and unhappily moved away.

"Here," he said to Page, patting the leather stool.

"Thank you so much," she said quietly, then slid onto the seat.

Standing beside her, he asked, "Can I be the first to buy you a drink?" his eyes eager.

She hesitated, not wanting to feel obligated to him. *Yet,* she thought, *it is still the way of the world to accept, no matter what the feminists say.* She politely agreed to "A martini with olive, please."

Roy waved to the bartender and, shouting above the noise he said, "Sammy, my man, a perfect martini for this perfect lady," and held up his empty glass. Sammy nodded at the order as Page blushed.

The drink arrived in front of her, a square, white cocktail napkin with the words, *Ping Ting Room* stamped on it.

Roy raised his glass to hers and said, "Well, as the Brits say, 'Cheers'," as he clinked her martini to his scotch and water, then poured the contents down his throat. Page heard the ice clink as they hit his teeth. He held up his glass to

Sammy, who nodded at the order.

Again with glass in hand, he said, "I'm Roy," as he held out his hand to shake.

She grasped his outstretched fingers and said, "I'm Page."

He brought her fingers to his lips, kissing them lightly, eyes glistening into hers and said, "Page huh? Like," crossing one hand over his heart, his head raised in mock performance, "a Page by any other name… oh, no, that's a rose," and he laughed.

Page smiled politely. She noted that Roy slurred his words. She wondered how long he'd been here tonight.

He pulled out his pack of cigarettes and offered one to her. This time, she took it. *Why not?* she thought, *I used to smoke before I got pregnant.* With that thought, an image of her newborn, tiny and precious, presented to her in the hospital popped into her head.

She leaned toward the flickering lighter and while drawing in the smoke, Page thought she heard cries of her first-born child. She waved away the smoke along with the memory.

The two exchanged mini stories about work, no mention of kids or divorce. She'd seen no ring on his finger, *but that means nothing*, she thought. *Men always remove their rings. As I've done tonight!* she gasped.

Roy told her he worked in aerospace, the Southern California "Gold Mine" industry, recently acclaimed for their efforts of setting the first man on the moon. Page listened intently as his eyes glowed, unsure if the glow was from passion for his craft or from alcohol. She thought, *I've gotten so bad at reading the signs lately.*

Page nodded politely as his words escalated, becoming slightly aggressive. As if pointing to the stars, Roy jabbed his glass toward the ceiling exclaiming, "A whole galaxy," swooping his glass across the ceiling, spilling it slightly on her dress.

"Oops," he said as he looked toward her lap. Page froze as he brushed his fingers over her dress, slowly, almost seductively, in his attempt to wipe away the water. Looking into her eyes, his pupils enlarged. Page wondered if he was also popping pills, or worse, becoming aroused.

His glass again empty, Roy motioned to Sammy, who stared at him for one moment longer than necessary. Roy's eyes narrowed, daring him to say, "No more."

Sammy, the Chinese emperor of his domain, had poured a thousand drinks for these suburban white folks and their offspring, when they'd come of age at twenty-one: a whole new generation beholden to him and to alcohol. Rarely did he stop serving a customer. Almost no one drove here since they lived nearby. But Sammy secretly poured more water atop the scotch and added ice. *At this point,* he mused, *he'll never know.*

"So," Roy said to her, a greasy smile curling his lips, "my pad is just around the corner and… I live alone."

She thought, *So?*

He added, "I've got a new waterbed… really comfortable…" He left the sentence unfinished, dangling between them.

Oh! she flinched, *he's asking me back to his place!* The image shot fear and alcohol simultaneously through her veins. Recovering from the shock, she stalled for time, murmuring, "Well, I've only had the one," holding up her empty glass.

Frowning, he reached for his wallet, its contents thin.

Perking up, she said, "I'll buy you one now."

He blustered, declining.

"No, really, feminism and all that," she said, attempting to sound assertive, placing her clutch purse on the bar and opening it.

"NO!" he shouted, then turned to his unseated friend. A hushed discussion and harsh words exchanged, then bills magically appearing between Roy's fingers.

Waving them at Sammy, he said, "Another," glancing down at her glass.

"Martini with olive," Sammy quietly finished the sentence. The men locked eyes, a line drawn in the sand.

Roy said, "And for me," dismissing him as he shoved another cigarette into his mouth and lighted it. In the glass ashtray beside him, smoke from the cigarette he'd left burning curled up and into his eyes. Cursing, he crushed it out.

Attempting to save his honor but unsure what to say, Page blurted out, "So, what plans do you have for the weekend?"

Immediately, she regretted her casual yet foolish remark. She watched as Roy's body, loose all evening, now became as rigid as a telephone pole.

Oh, no! she gasped, *now he'll think I want future dates plans and obligations, marriage!*

He fumbled for another cigarette, then noticing he already had one going between his fingers, attempted to casually draw out the smoke. Roy was speechless.

Page scrambled to change the subject but could think of nothing to say. Not kids or divorce, not work, or the sleazy, little man at the tract housing development.

His eyes hovered above hers, wide in fear, peering through the smoke into the crowd and scanning, desperate in their search, for a friend or another woman perhaps, any way to escape.

Lamely, she said, "I'm thinking of taking a pottery course."

Page sat blank as he replied distractedly, "Hmmm? Pottery? That's like... with pots, right?"

"Right," she said and nothing more.
Rising, he said, "Sorry, nature calls," Staggering through the back of the bar, Roy veered to the left, became entangled in the beaded curtain, cursed, then stumbled toward the men's room.

Page sat alone, sipping the remains of her martini. She nibbled at the olive on its toothpick, then placed it on the napkin.

Looking into the mirror above the bar, its colorful bottles happily shining, she thought, *What the heck am I doing here anyway? To find a man to replace the one who left me? No, not that,* shaking her head. *I came to be in a crowd different from the one I no longer feel I belong in anymore. The neighborhood barbecues with women clustered around me, chatting only about their kids and their husbands. The men, gathered in collective brotherhood, barking about real world problems. Drinking too much, pinching one of our asses, a boyish snicker and shrug as explanation. Why did none of us ever object? Do all women only shrug it off? Or is it only in the suburbs?* Then she thought, *Is this any different?*

She studied the crowds in the mirror. The aerospace crew had left, but carbon copy faces replaced them. Some dressed in short-sleeved shirts with Hawaiian flowers, gray-belted in loose trousers. Others wore tieless shirts paired with ironed jeans. The men stood beside their wives or not wives. Only Sammy knew who was married, recently divorced or here on a tryst.

Never showing a hint of interest, he'd watch discreetly and listen intently while blending foaming concoctions of the Orient. He poured the liquid into deep-bowled glasses: rum and snowy white coconut cocktails, topped with a slice of juicy pineapple, a plump red cherry, and tiny paper umbrella.

Sammy was the favorite of lonely singles and divorcees, the women clustering at the bar, giggling at his jokes, all intuitively knowing him to be a thoughtful man of integrity.

The men guffawed and secretly motioned behind the back of the women with a wink to Sammy, to strengthen their women's drinks. Sammy never did.

Page watched silently and listened to the shrieks of laughter, the men's low tenors baiting and joking, the clicking of glasses and merriment surrounding her.

She thought again of the parties with her neighbors. She'd watched as her friend's boys grew from smiling kids to teens. The fraternity of men encircling them, thrusting beers into their hands, snickering at jokes deemed too offensive for women's ears.

She thought, *Am I bringing up my sons to be this way? What was mimicking these men doing to them? Have I raised them to treat young women with courtesy and respect? Or will they become another generation of men who'll do as they always have? Drink, then show disrespect and apathy towards their wives? And what of my daughter? Was this teaching her not only to expect such behavior but accept it?*

Page turned from the mirror to glance down at her watch: a tiny, precious, rhinestone Timex. Her children had pooled all their money to buy it for her on the first Mother's Day after the divorce from their father.

What a strange, grateful day that had been with the kids. All practically grown-up now, she sighed. *They'd made it so special with breakfast: French toast cooked by my precious daughter, Joni. Too much salt, but otherwise delicious. And the twins, Pat and Mike, seeming so grown up, acting like waiters with dish towels draped over their arms.*

All three of them dressed so nicely for once, not even for church but for me.

Page watched as the tiny hand swept the minutes from 5 to 10. Glancing towards the back of the bar, she just caught sight of Roy stumbling out the back door, into the alley and out of her life.

She looked up into Sammy's deep brown eyes focused on her own. They did not speak. Then she said, "Well, Sammy, one for the road?" as she pulled a bill from her clutch purse. Sammy nodded as he thrust the scoop into the ice.

Kay

Dressed in a bright, colorful, sleeveless dress, Kay sat at the bar, killing time by reminiscing about her crazy life. The wild days of parties and drugs now behind her, she recalled them tonight with clarity.

Back in the day, she mused, *I was up for anything. Booze and pot of course, sometimes LSD and sex with anyone at those swinging singles parties. The ones up the coast on the beach were the best. Huh! A far cry from the Annette Funicello and Frankie Avalon movies I'd watched a few years before.* Kay chuckled to herself, *Ah, those were the days - free love.*

A young woman squeezed up to the bar, trying to wave for the bartender. Kay turned to her, smiled and said, "You've got to shout to get Sammy's attention." Then she yelled, "Sammy! Order here!" He came and took her order.

"Thanks," she said.

"Sure," she said, then thought, *She looks so much like Sara.* The girl noticed her gaze. Kay said, "Sorry… I didn't mean to stare. It's just… you remind me of someone."

The girl paid for her drink then said, "Well, thanks again," and walked away.

Kay remembered the sweet face of her sister, Sara,

her innocent smile, falling in love at sixteen. The memory of their last conversation came flooding back to her.

I tried to talk to her about sex in a realistic way. I gave her condoms... she was disgusted and pushed them away. "Honey, please listen, this is serious. You want to end up like Mom? Pregnant? Marrying a guy she doesn't even like?"

"I'm not Mom! She's a slut!"

"She's not a slut. She just thought she was in love. When she got pregnant, the guy hopped on his motorcycle and sped out of town. Yes, our father left her. Like this boy will do to you."

"He loves me," she said softly.

"But will he still love you tomorrow? *I quoted lyrics from The Shirelles.*

"Don't!" she shouted. "I love that song!"

"Do you know what that tune is about?"

"It's about love."

"Yes, love... and sex. That Catch 22 plight girls have about whether to sleep with a guy or not. And what will happen to you when you do that? You'll be left pregnant and alone."

"You'd leave me?" she asked, frightened.

"No! Of course not! So let's just not let that happen,

okay? Honey, I know girls who got pregnant - it was horrible… backroom abortions…"

"Don't! Don't you dare bring this into my head! It's my life, not yours! You haven't been around since I was twelve. You were out doing God knows what? Pretending in a fog of weed that everything was great! While I went to school, you got stoned. Why would I listen to you?"

I bit back my defenses and said, "You're right. I messed up. But I'm not doing that shit anymore. I'm here for you now."

Sara's eyes flashed as she said, "It's too late. I don't want a sister I can't count on."

A place inside my heart cracked then. I wanted to tell her the dangers, how to protect herself but when I looked into her eyes, I saw a closed door. I said, "You can count on me. Look, I won't tell you how to live your life. It's just that I know stuff you don't know yet. It's stuff you really need to know."

"I'll find out from my friends or on my own… without you."

"Okay, just promise me one thing, okay?" She shrugged.

"Promise if you ever need help, if you get pregnant… you'll come to me. Promise."

"I'm not gonna get pregnant."

"Okay, just promise me."

"I promise," then she walked away.

But she didn't come to me.

Kay wanted to bang her fist on the bar and throw her glass at the mirror.

She remembered the night the cops came. Sara, in the hospital with internal bleeding. Botched abortion. She didn't make it.

Kay gulped her drink, then thought, *Mom somehow got money for a decent burial… money from an uncle I never heard of. Probably one of her ex-lovers.*

We stood and cried as the casket was put in the ground. I cried for weeks, then never again. Damn it! Sara never told me the guy ran out, or that she was pregnant. I could have found her a good place, not the shithole she'd gone to. Poor kid, she must have been terrified. I was an ass not to take better care of her, to make sure she'd be careful. Free love… yeah, right! Not for Sara, not for any woman. Only free for guys, with no legal responsibility. If I ever find that punk, I'll…

Sammy asked if she wanted a drink. She smiled and nodded yes. As he placed it in front of her, she recalled the women she'd met at city college in the years before the tragedy.

Women there talked about Women's Liberation. Not for me, I'd thought at the time. I'd been too busy getting high, fighting in political groups with hippies in San Francisco.

She remembered them, *stoned and screaming, "Fight the establishment! End the war!" Huh!* Kay thought, *their only experience of war had been as kids, playing with G.I. Joe dolls.*

She recalled meeting a serviceman on leave at a party in Topanga. *We were just hanging out, getting high. Then some of the hippies pointed to his crewcut and yelled, "Baby burner!"*

I froze in shock, then yelled, "What the hell do you know? You've never even seen a war!" The soldier got furious at them but also at me! Me and my big mouth, she thought. *In my defense of him, I instead humiliated him.*

Hell, she rebuked herself, *I'm one to talk. At least the hippies yelled against the brutality of war. I agreed with that. That's why I joined them in the first place. Plus, a lot of them were scared stiff to be drafted... they still are. I'd sympathized, of course. Who in their right mind wanted to kill?*

My friends started backing off me then... but those protest parties had become a drag anyway. They did teach me one thing though: that those men thought a woman was created for two things and nothing else: cooking or sex. Our votes weren't even counted, much less, listened to. After that, I'd wander off, sometimes taking a woman to my bed.

Kay thought of her first time with a woman: *The invitation of a bright smile. Like a surprise without knowing or thinking I wanted her. She pauses, holding my eyes with hers. Looks down at my lips. A rush zips up my spine. She kisses me gently, not briefly, not yet passionately. Her fingers stroke the back of my neck, pulling from inside me a fire. Fingers lightly trace my skin. A bath of warmth I kiss, dive into, flying through me. I stretch to feel her inside, a wave of control I give into, longing for the violent rush I know but never knew. The slam, crash, shivering lust. Wet, wondrous, my heart slams in my chest. I lie down, her skin pressed to mine, sweating, floating, perfect. My heart simmers, slowly purring. I rest, then sleep into the night. The world around me no longer real. But inside, I glow.*

Kay sipped her drink lazily, savoring the flavor. Then remembered *if one of the guys got horny and started nosing around, I'd scream, "Get out! You won't listen to my opinions? Then no sex for you!" He'd freaked out of course. But usually, he won over a woman, taking her to his bed. Fuck this, I'm outta here... I'd said and moved here to L.A., getting a cheap place in town.* Their hypocrisy infuriated her.

Still, she mused, *I did meet the love of my life, well, what I thought was love at the time anyway, at that party up the coast. He practically swept me off my feet with his dreamy eyes, making out in the sand. We married soon after. But that hadn't worked out either... turned out he was a loser,* she thought, although she understood why. His father was a real bastard.

As the weeks became months, Kay saw his steady amount of drinking and flirting hadn't stopped with her. *He disappeared late nights and weekends for "a second job" he said. How stupid did he think I was!?!*

Kay filed for divorce then began to explore her own sexual desires. Now she was almost proud of the word, "Lesbian" whispered about her. *Hell,* she thought, *most people here know but don't dare say, not to my face. Maybe that's why I bonded so well with "The Dragon Lady."*

I ran into June in a woman's bar on Cahuenga Boulevard. She had a sweet, young woman with her, obviously crazy about her, Kay remembered *and apparently, the affection was mutual.*

We drank shots, swapped stories and laughed 'til the bar closed. Wow! Who knew June was so fun, so different from the face she puts on here, then she thought, *and for me?* Kay glanced up at her reflection in the mirror, then further down the bar.

The Meeting

Kay watched as Roy walked right past her without even a glance, stumbled toward the men's room, then escaped out the back door.

Bastard! she cursed, *he left me when I went to the ladies room, presumedly for a pack of smokes and, of course, he got infatuated with that brunette over there, forgetting our conversation completely.*

That's what I get, she grumbled, *for my noble efforts to permanently let him off his alimony payments. Completely ludicrous,* she thought, *since he just blew it on that brunette over there and apparently walked out on her too.*

Her hazel eyes now focused, slightly irritated but oddly curious about the brunette. *She is beautiful* Kay thought to herself, *Roy always did have good taste.*

When a man rose and left the bar, a seat next to the brunette came free. Kay rose and moved next to her. Turning towards her she said, "No luck, huh?"

Page, oblivious, did not reply.

Kay repeated her words, "No luck, huh?"

Page turned to her and said, "Excuse me? Were you speaking to me?"

"Yes, I was," she said, her eyes locked on her. She

repeated, "I said, 'no luck, huh?'"

Page blinked, trying to make sense of the comment, then said, "I don't know what you mean… luck?"

Kay answered, "No luck… with Roy…"

Page blinked again. She sensed being chastised for something, but for what? She hadn't a clue. Page stiffened when the fog finally lifted and said, "Oh, you were what? Watching us? You know Roy then? He's a friend of yours?"

"Mmmm," she replied, "A friend. Yes…I guess that's what he is and also… my husband."

"Oh!" she exclaimed, red-faced in embarrassment. Images of her ex-husband's infidelity, her own words thrown as weapons at him about "the other woman" ran through her head. *And now,* she thought, *that other woman is… me!*

Kay said, "Hey, it's okay," shocked at Page's crimson face, suddenly ashamed. She said "I'm sorry. Yes, Roy is… *was* my husband… we're divorced."

Page's brow now eased but still, she felt wronged, unjustly accused. *But,* she thought, *I accused myself.* As the air floated thick with tension between the two women, Sammy appeared suddenly before them, setting Page's martini in front of her. She opened her clutch purse, then paused, turned to the woman, and said, "Look, would you… can I buy you a drink? On me? It's the least I can do."

The woman mused, *Well, Roy just spent my alimony on her so...* She playfully replied, "Sure, why not? Another martini please, Sammy."

He nodded and turned towards his task. As the drink was placed in front of her, she said, "Thanks, Sammy. Do you know, sorry," turning to Page, she asked, "what was your name?"

"Page Dubois," she replied, "And you are?"

"I'm Kay. Kay Fitzgerald. Sammy, this is Page. Page... Sammy."

"Very pleased to meet you Ms. Dubois," Sammy smiled, then said, "I hope you are enjoying your drink?"

Page replied, "Oh, yes, very much! It's just right." Sammy nodded approval, turning toward another customer.

The women raised their glasses. Then Kay said, "Thank you," as their glasses rang out.

"I'm sorry about Roy," they said in unison, then laughed.

Page said, "No, Kay, I'm so embarrassed! I'm just no good at this all..." as her eyes scanned the room, focusing on the couples, the wordless seductions, the pick-ups.

Kay said, "The singles scene, you mean?"

"Yes," Page replied, "it's all so new and..."

"Sordid?"

Page eased her shoulders and said, "Yes. Sordid, that's the word. I've not been out in years."

"Divorced?" Kay asked boldly.

Page's gray eyes misted over. She said, "Yes. Kind of recently… a year ago."

Kay's brown eyes softened at Page's grief. She said, "I know, I've been through it…" She put a hand over Page's. "It'll get easier though."

Page tensed, squeezed it, then reached for her glass.

Kay sipped her drink, changing the subject and asked, "Do you have children?"

Page lit up. "Yes!" she said, "Three: a girl and two boys, twins."

"Wow!" Kay exclaimed, "That's a handful. Are they still young?"

"Yes, well, no." Laughing, she explained, "They're almost in high school, practically out of the house now… Do you have kids?"

Kay shook her head no.

Page asked, "Do you work?"

Kay said "Yes, as a cashier at the market. Before that, I worked as a waitress to pay for city college. I didn't like it much. The guys said stuff like, 'You're so pretty! A face like yours should smile more.' I quit after a few weeks. I felt too much like a performing seal." Kay chuckled, then asked, "Do you work?"

"Yes," Page replied, "I took an exam for a realtor's license a few months ago. You know, with male colleagues showing me the ropes, but…"

"But?"

"But I don't think they like working with women."

Kay said, "Ahhh, playing games, huh?"

Page answered, "Not maliciously I don't think, I hope not, just a bit… playful."

"Playful, how?" Kay asked.

Page told her about "The Chalet" in the Hollywood Hills and they burst out laughing.

Page said, "They gave me the crummiest house to sell."

Kay paused. Brightening she said, "So! A challenge then."

Page smiled, "Yes, that's right… a challenge."

"Well, girl," Kay said, "It's not easy but you'll survive."

Page smiled at Kay, filled suddenly with a joyous sisterhood she'd never known. She said, "Yes! I will survive."

"Thatta girl!" Kay exclaimed, then held her glass up to toast. "Here's to Women's Liberation!"

Page hesitated, then clicked her glass.

Kay said, "Women's Lib… not your thing?"

"Mmmm, no," Page replied, "It's not that, it's just… so new, so strange… Like I've been living in a bubble for years."

"You were raising three great kids," Kay said.

Page smiled. "Thanks," she said. "Still, I'm curious, do you, are you involved in… it?"

"Hell, yes!" Kay exclaimed and Page giggled.

Kay continued, "It's like this… my first year at city college, I met Roy at a 'free love' party up the coast."

Page's eyes became round in surprise. "Free… love party?"

"Come on," Kay said, "Ya know… mingling couples, where no one is with anyone… wife swapping, stuff like that, you know… or… do you?"

Page nodded, unsure, while thinking, *I've heard rumors about such things, so… they really do exist,* then said, "So, how was… that?"

"Well, fine," Kay continued, "I saw Roy there and well, he can be a stinker, but wow! Those bedroom eyes!" Page blushed.

"We drifted up the beach and… well…"

"Yes!" said Page, cutting her off and laughing, "I can

imagine that! And then?"

"Then we just hit it off. We saw each other for a few months, and then he completely floored me with a marriage proposal! It was really just to get me on the pill. The doctor said I needed a 'note from my fiancé' Can you believe that?"

Page nodded. She had needed one too.

Kay said, "To think a woman needs a note from a man for permission to control her own body! It's so insulting!"

Kay remembered women she'd known who'd become pregnant. That news sent their "mates" scurrying for the hills, leaving the women to wrestle with their consciences while pondering their only two options: an illegal abortion in a filthy back room or leaving their youth and dignity behind to have the kid, by going to a convent, then giving it up for adoption. They'd not been financially able to keep the kid, even if they'd wanted to. In place of sympathy, they'd instead earned the loathing of their families, who'd held their good name in society more important than their daughter or grandchild. These women mourned the loss of their child while fighting the stigma ever since. *The religious hypocrites can preach all they want,* Kay thought, *but they'll never pay for an unwanted child.*

Kay had ensured no pregnancy for herself by always keeping condoms with her. She knew that was illegal too. To be caught by police with condoms in her purse would get her an arrest for prostitution. But she hadn't trusted men to be responsible for what would end up being her problem alone.

Then she said, "That's one reason I got interested in Woman's Lib. It finally dawned on me that the whole 'free love' thing is an excuse for men to get free sex. It can't be free when only one half gets it for free. Anyway, so Roy and I got hitched at Town Hall. But soon after that I came to know the real Roy."

Page looked at her, questioning.

"Well," she continued, "you've seen he likes to drink, well, *loves* to drink."

Page nodded.

"Did he tell you he worked in aerospace?"

"Yes," Page answered, "he seems quite dedicated."

"Mmmm, I thought so… he uses that line a lot. Fact is, he's not."

Page jolted in surprise.

"Oh," she continued, "he works in aerospace, all right… as a janitor." Kay nodded her head, "It's true." She did not mention he also flunked out of high school. "His drinking and sexual romps - yep, he cheated on me, were too tempting for him. I tried to get him into AA, then couples therapy, even meditation... he wouldn't go for it. I saw I couldn't help him anymore. After five months of marriage, I filed for a divorce. Still, he's a good guy..."

Page's face showed shock at the ridiculous deception but also, she suddenly felt sorry for him. She sipped her drink, meditatively. Then, carefully setting Roy, women's issues, and the inner conflict she still felt about her own divorce aside, she said, "So, you divorced and then what? The time for yourself I mean, what did you come up with? Tell me more... about you."

"Me?" Kay said, "Not a lot there. I tried studying painting and photography at city college. That didn't get me very far."

Impressed, Page said, "Wow! I've always wanted to learn those."

Kay sipped her drink, then held her eyes and said, "Also, I'm lesbian."

Page did not look away.

"Yep, it's true. I finally realized this - though I've hid it a long time... since I was a kid."

Page said, "But you were…"

"Married?" Kay answered, "No, it's not because of Roy. It's just who I am, who I've always been. These days, free sex, it's been a nice ride but… Dammit! Marriage is what society expects, right?"

Page nodded, unintentionally.

"Most of them," she began looking around at the couples, "know or suspect. They never dare say 'Lezzie' to my face but I'm sure they all think it. And you know what? That's fine with me."

Her eyes looked into Page's, standing her ground but also slightly fearful of the question she dared not ask, poised on her lips - *Will it be okay with you?*

Page looked at her, understanding the unspoken question. She squeezed Kay's hand, smiled, then said, "You're my friend, Kay. Now, tell me more about you, about what you do. What happened with college?"

"Mmm," Kay replied, "turns out I got more from the Women's Movement than art instruction. Hell, I don't have it so bad: no kids and Roy pays me alimony… but had he not run out on me tonight, he would have learned that he no longer needs to pay me."

Page's eyebrows flew up instinctively, anticipating another story of a marriage proposal, then remembered this was highly unlikely.

Kay said, "I just don't feel okay to take money from him anymore. Hell, I don't have it so bad, my rent is about a hundred bucks, my car is old but runs well, my bills are almost nothing and my salary pays for it all okay. Besides… he'd rather spend money on you! Ha! Just kidding! I did see him looking like a deer caught in headlights though and thought, Uh oh… cornered."

"I hadn't cornered him," Page replied, "I only asked what plans he had for the weekend. Stupid, I know."

Kay laughed, then said, "I know Page… I just know him so well. If he wasn't so paranoid, you two might have hit it off… my inside gossip hasn't helped."

"No," Page said, "I'm done dating for now. Maybe when the kids leave."

"Well, don't sell yourself short," Kay replied, "You're still young, and very beautiful… Besides," noting Page's discomfort, "Not all men are stinkers… just most of them. Ha! Just kidding!"

Mrs. Cheng came through the beaded curtains.

Page leaned in toward Kay and whispered, "Do you know her? You heard she's the owner on this place now, right?"

Kay nodded, tensing at the gossip and said, "She's a friend of mine…"

"Oh! I didn't mean anything by it… I know the name they call her is awful… I'd never use it… I didn't mean to… I just admire her so much… I think she's my hero. But I just wondered how that name ever got started."

To Page's shock, Kay raised her hand and called over "The Dragon Lady."

"No… don't!" Page exclaimed in fear.

Kay shushed her as she walked up to them.

"Hello, Kay," she said. Her eyes looked tired. Speaking to Sammy, she said, "Almost closing time, Sammy."

He nodded, turned from them, and shouted, "Last call!" The customers rushed to the bar, hands grasping empty glasses. Sammy quickly began mixing their orders.

Turning back to the women, Mrs. Cheng said, "Yes, Kay, you were saying?" But her jade eyes were looking at Page.

Kay said, "This is Page - Page, this is June… or maybe I should say, 'The Dragon Lady.'"

Page was mortified, but the two women just laughed.

Kay continued, "Page was wondering how you got that name."

Page exclaimed, "No… I… I'm not… I just admire you so much… I mean, a woman, the owner of this wonderful place." Page looked at her, wracked with fear that she'd offended her.

June paused, looking at Kay, then smiled and sat down. In a quiet voice, she said, "Call me June. That name was from when I was in the pictures."

Page exclaimed, "The movies you mean? Really?" Page had never met an actress before.

June said, "Ahh… a long time, too long ago. Yes, at sixteen, they'd made me a star, but then…" she laughed, "they didn't know what to do with me."

Page looked puzzled.

June said, "All the Chinese roles were given to anyone except a Chinese. Germans mostly, but American Indians and Hungarians as well."

Page was appalled. She said. "But that's not…"

"Fair?" June answered, "no. It definitely isn't. But Hollywood isn't fair, just profitable. But there was no excuse for it, there still isn't."

Kay piped up, "Tell her about the name."

June said, "Ahh, yes. The name. Typical… Only 'The Dragon Lady' or 'Butterfly' was ever written by critics regarding my one lead role. Still… it was an exciting time for me."

Page watched as June's green eyes softened in memory. Turning to Sammy, June said, "Give these two a martini on me. I'll have one too… after the crowd leaves."

The women turned to watch people as they downed their drinks, Sammy refusing their pleas of, "Just one more… *please?*" Wiping the bar, he said, "No more, sorry. Next time."

The crowds grumpily dispersed as Mrs. Cheng rose and led them through the beaded curtain, locking the front door. Dimming the lights to avoid the police, she returned to her seat, held up her glass, then said, "Well, here's to what might have been." With that, they clinked her glass.

She turned to Sammy and said, "Get one for yourself, Sammy. I'm feeling like a star tonight."

As the three women chatted, suddenly, Roy appeared through the back door. Mrs. Cheng cursed herself for forgetting to lock it as she watched him stumble toward them.

Focusing on Kay, he said, "Hi, Kay. Hey!" His eyes moving with effort, attempting to focus on Page, he exclaimed, "Hey…" wagging his finger at her, "I know you." Then looking between the two women, he said, "You… you're not… oh, hell, not you too?! Christ, what's the world coming to?!" Then to Sammy, he barked, "I need a drink!"

Kay tensed, then said, "No, Roy, she's not… another one. But with you as an alternative?"

Roy frowned at her as she said, "No more booze for you. You've drank it all up."

He snapped, "You're not my wife anymore, like you ever were," then slumped against her and said, "What's wrong with me, anyway, huh? Whatcha want with women, anyway?"

"Probably the same things you do Roy." Then, affectionately, she said, "Come on, I'll walk you home."

Sammy came from behind the bar, put his hand on Roy's shoulder and said, "No. I will drive you home. Goodnight, ladies."

The women replied, "Good night, Sammy and thanks!"

They watched as Sammy steered Roy through the back door. Mrs. Cheng locked the door behind them and sat down. Looking at each other, they smiled.

The next morning, the kids were awake, busy with cereal for breakfast and plans for the day.

Page came in, a bit foggy, which was commented upon by her sons and daughter.

"Kinda late last night, huh, Mom?" said her son, Mike. "Yeah," the twin Pat said, "where did ya go?"

Her daughter, Joni said, "You okay, Mom? Everything go all right?"

"Yes," she answered them, "I went to our old stomping grounds, House of Cheng."

"Yum!" they cried out in unison.

"Let's go there again soon. I love their sticky ribs!" Pat chimed in.

She watched as they dispersed for the day while she made a pot of coffee. Mike returned hesitantly.

"Hi again," she said to him, "What's up?"

He stalled, then it all came out in a rush. "I know you don't really like me to have them, but I have a *Playboy* magazine under my bed. *I know, I know,* but I read the articles. Dad showed me. I did have one. A *Playboy* I mean, but now it's missing. I asked Pat but he didn't take it. But then I went into Joni's room, and… well… I caught HER looking at it. That's kinda weird, huh?" he said, looking at her.

Page was surprised and unsure what to say so said, "You shouldn't have that! You're not old enough. It figures your father gave you that!" she grumbled.

He tried to get his father out of trouble now by saying, "It's kinda weird that Joni was lookin' at it, huh, Mom?"

She answered, "I'll talk to her about it. Aren't you supposed to be at the baseball game?" He yelped and ran out of the apartment.

She sipped her coffee, trying to figure out why on earth her daughter would want to look at that.

When Joni came in, she said, "Honey, sit down a minute, okay?"

"But I'm due at the library at noon," she replied.

Page said, "I know, just for a few minutes."

Joni sat down, looking at her.

Page began, "Honey, I know now is a difficult time for you… going into high school, starting new classes. Maybe you're trying to fit in and that's natural to want to… but… did you maybe look at photographs of women, who are older to give you ideas how to look? Because honey, the photographs in that *Playboy* magazine are not real, they're air brushed to look that way. Real women don't look like that.…"

Joni stared at her, embarrassed she'd been caught. Then she looked her straight in the eye and said, "But Mom, I don't want to look like them or be like them… I want to *be with them*. Understand? Mom, I'm lesbian."

This novelette is dedicated to all the men who have been lost to us and the world.

The Gold Ring

by Chantz Perkins

THE GOLD RING

By

CHANTZ PERKINS

The Gold Ring

Frustratin' Day

On the Embarcadero

Gregg

Paul

A Very Practical Solution

Cracks in Paradise

Fear in the Air

The Farewell

Frustratin' Day

Paul entered his apartment and tossed his keys on the table. On the floor, an empty bottle of wine rolled on its side as a full ashtray lightly blew ashes across the table and onto the bed. An open window had scattered sketches all over the floor where he'd dropped them a few nights ago. He'd fallen into bed, disgusted.

Bending to pick them up, he thought, *No, the sketches aren't right because I have no idea of who or what this icon should be.*

The boss at his new ad firm had said, "We need a new icon for the American housewife. The product? A fast, strong and easy power cleaner that will clean up anything. FAST AND STRONG AND EASY! These are the big features, and the icon has to say that."

Paul had an aversion to the way his new boss viewed creating images - easy as opening a bottle of Chardonnay.

In frustration, Paul tossed on jeans, a T-shirt, and slipped brown loafers onto his bare feet. He closed his door in search of a drink. Living in West Hollywood had its advantages. Bars, a lot of them and close by. He walked along Fountain Avenue. The sky was just turning from pink to twilight as he came to the corner of Santa Monica Boulevard, entering Revolver bar. He went through the door and squinted into the darkness. He glanced around at the silhouettes. Some lively and chattering in groups, some in twos, their eyes only on each other.

Paul walked up to the bar and slid onto a stool. The boy behind the bar turned towards him sliding a coaster before him. His eyes showed his youth and boredom.

"Yeah?" he said.

Paul smiled at him and said, "Just a Corona please."

Paul watched as the boy turned and took a beer out of the fridge, flipped off the cap and put it in front of him. Turning his back on Paul's "Thank you," he began to fiddle with the music.

The tune of *Hot, Hot, Hot*, tinkled to a Caribbean beat in unison with the colored lights hanging above them.

Looking into the mirror behind the bar in front of him, Paul just caught sight of a man to his right, watching him.

Paul thought he recognized the man, then it hit him. He was an on again, off again character actor, whom he'd seen in films, B ones. He had massive arms, a tight, black T-shirt and huge thighs that bulged in his tight, white pants. He also possessed the looks to scare the life out of you - not because he was ugly - far from it - but because he held the menacing look of a bouncer at a bar: the kind that smashed heads together.

Paul watched him in the mirror until getting caught by him - their eyes locking for that one second too long. Paul turned boldly towards him, smiling and said, "You terrified me in every movie I've seen you in."

Paul was sure he'd seen the fellow blush, his tanned, domed head darkening. Then he grinned, all menacing looks softening like the morning sun cracking the dawn.

"Why, thanks," he said with slightly Southern drawl, moving to a seat next to him. "I'm Brad," he said, extending his hand to shake.

He replied, "I'm Paul." Gripping his hand, Paul winced, just a little.

They chatted in all the opening lines one says in politeness: Where are you from? When did you move here? What do you do for work? Paul spoke of his recent move to Los Angeles, a new job at an advertising agency, the current project, and the reason he'd come to be in the bar tonight.

"Frustratin', huh? Being an artist," Brad said in sympathy, "creating a painting and then letting it go. Like losing your first love. I used to paint myself."

Paul watched as Brad fingered a gold earring on his left ear, thoughtlessly turning it round and round, round and round.

Paul's mind drifted back to a hospital waiting room in another city. He knew his partner of three years lay in the room next to this one, dying.

Across from him sat the man's mother. They had never spoken. Now and then, she eyed him suspiciously but said nothing. She had not known her son was gay, nor had she wanted to.

On the Embarcadero

White clouds floated like dancing children hand in hand across the crisp blue San Francisco sky.

Paul sat bundled in his dirty leather jacket, paint-splattered, baggy jeans and tennis shoes. He watched the trees sway in the breeze as he sketched the people dotted around him at the Cat Café on the Embarcadero.

His concentration was pierced suddenly by a high-pitched shriek of indignation. Looking toward the source, he noticed a group of young men sitting on the terrace across from him.

They were in their mid-twenties, like him. But unlike him, they were dressed in expensive, long wool coats and around their necks, colorful mufflers.

The shriek had come from an older man who sat encircled by them, the obvious focus of their youthful admiration.

The man was high cheek-boned, with a classic straight nose. Very distinguished. His face had a Garboesque quality that seemed to defy age, which Paul summed up to be just the other side of thirty-nine. His amber hair was worn long, brushed up and off his brow, falling just over the collar of his blazer, which Paul thought, *Expensive, but too thin.*

Completely impractical for this cold weather. Then, *It is stunning though, how its metallic shimmer of blue-green sets off the emerald of his piercing green eyes.*

Speaking with a childlike enthusiasm, the man shrieked, "I did not fondle him under the table!" as his eyes surveyed the surrounding families, pleased at their disapproving glances. He made a point to smile at each and every one of them.

One of his friends said, "Oh, come ON, Gregg, *you did*!"

"No!" the man stated firmly, then leaned back and demurely said, "I was merely stroking his leg under the table, consoling him really. After all, his lover had just died for Christ's sake."

Paul watched as the group fell silent.

The man became irritated at the sudden gloom now hovering over the table. He began to fan his face as if clearing poison from the air.

"After all," he continued while his voice transitioned into the melodic tone of a seductive Southern belle, "I've always depended on the *kindness* of strangers…"

The men roared in laughter. Tennessee's line had again worked its magic. One of them chirped, "Yeah, sure,

Gregg, you consoled him all right… right into the men's toilet!"

Laughter again erupted as the man giggled. Paul watched, amazed. He'd never seen anyone so comfortable in their skin.

Paul's fascination had not gone unnoticed. The man glanced over at him, rose from his chair, and to his surprise, walked straight over to his table.

Pulling out a chair, he sat directly in front of him, elbows on the table, piercing green eyes staring straight into his.

"I haven't seen you before," he said.

"No," Paul stammered, trying to find his voice, "I've… I've not been out much."

"Oooo, really?," the man eagerly inquired, "Why is that?"

"I, um," Paul swallowed, "I've been working…" his voice trailing away.

"*Working?*" he said as though suddenly detecting a putrid smell. Then, feigning interest, he asked, "Uh huh… really? What are you working on?"

His eyes snapped from Paul's toward the sketchbook in front of him. "What have you got here?" and he snatched the book from him. Looking at it, he exclaimed, "Is this *moi*?

Why, I look gorgeous!" He seemed genuinely flattered but tried not to show it.

"Well," Paul began, relaxing into his element, "It's just a sketch."

"Yes, I see," the man said dismissively but still curious. Then, "Well, if you ever need a model…"

He plucked the pencil out of Paul's hand, and with a flourish, he wrote something and pushed it back.

Paul looked down. In cursive, flamboyant hand, he'd written *Gregg Stanford* and a phone number across the bottom of the page. He raised his head to respond but Gregg had already sashayed from him, his fingers raised in a wiggle of farewell.

Paul watched as Gregg returned to his entourage, met with whispered inquiry upon his return. Shushing them, he smoothly segued the conversation toward one of the boys and, perhaps for the first time in his life, away from himself.

Gregg

Born from the blue blood stock of San Francisco's elite, Gregg lived in a mansion overlooking the city with his mother and a flock of servants, all of whom were aware of Gregg's preference for men, though none dared ever speak of it. Neither had the guests to the mansion, who instead remained discreet, curious, and suspicious.

Only his mother, who still insisted on calling him Gregory would refer to "that nice girl whom I met at the luncheon, the daughter of – what was their name? A lovely girl, quite a catch really."

Eagerly, she'd await any glimmer of interest from her son.

When his reply was only an enthusiastic reading from the current best seller, she'd slump, ever so slightly, in defeat.

Looking at him, a slight confusion would cross her features as a shimmer of thought, one that always came after these sessions with Gregory, would attempt to form inside her head. That Gregory might be, *that way*.

Slowly, feelings that she'd tried for years to ignore, began to taunt her, whispering *it's probably all your fault*.

She thought back on her marriage to Gregory's father, a weak, unimaginative sort of man.

Soon after Gregory's university graduation, she'd filed for divorce, stolen and then sold his company, keeping the mansion, the servants, and Gregory for herself.

And yet, the blame, which tried for years to poke her subconscious with their shards of truth, could not stand up to her for long. Instead, it grew fearful, bowing and retreating as a chastised servant. *Why I ever married that man I'll never know.* Her attention now focused on the menu, she left in search of the cook.

Gregg glanced up from his novel, chuckling at this mother's bewilderment. He rose and walked to the window. Gazing out, he saw antique mansions of old mixed with sharp-cornered high-rises slashing the blue sky, and in the distance, the sea sparkling.

Magnificent, he groaned, *as always.*

"God! Won't she ever just *shut up?*" he said aloud, throwing his book onto the couch. *She'll never understand,* he thought, *that for me, men are tantalizing young boys, sitting at their master's feet, just out of reach. And girls? Well, girls just simply fade away, like the lines from a badly written novel.*

Gregg thought back to his years at an Ivy League University, his studies exclusively literature. Barely passing other subjects, he had somehow squeezed through to graduation.

How had I done that? he wondered. He suspected his mother's influence. *Donation of a new wing most likely. She probably controlled that too...* he thought with a groan. Then, as with all that bored him, he quickly dismissed the idea.

Gregg was brilliant and without a drop of self-discipline.

Paul

Paul was raised in the low-income area of Oakland.

From an early age, his talents in the arts, though tremendous, had not included reality. He'd finally come to the realization that his dream of living the life of an artist in Paris lacked any practicality. He had barely passed French courses or any other language for that matter. He searched his brain for an alternative, one that would not leave him starving on a Parisian street.

His idea of a career in fashion illustration had not gone over well with his parents.

His father roared, "Fashion?! That's for girls! The only men in fashion should be truckers, delivering goods. All others are pansies!" eyeing Paul suspiciously.

Paul hadn't the slightest notion why he was such a huge disappointment to his father, who was like a Greek god to him. An ex-Marine, big and powerful in work and drink. *He* had made *his mark in the world* by fighting proudly, serving as a gunner on a battleship in World War II, like his father had fought before him, in the Great War.

Paul spent his childhood listening to his father's tales of glory, *"Shooting down the kamikaze nip bastards,"* as they zeroed toward him, the deafening noise and screams of battle booming in his ears.

For Paul, who had grown up playing with G.I. Joe dolls and model airplanes, these tales of bravery were merely boyhood fantasies. When the Vietnam War came along, he'd been too young for the draft.

Paul couldn't even stomach watching the news on their black and white TV or gazing into *Life* magazine for fear of seeing yet another photograph of soldiers, rifles raised, trudging through the jungle in mud-covered fatigues. Or worse, images of young Vietnamese girls, their tiny bodies wet and naked, screaming from the burn of a napalm attack.

It had been in high school by classmates that Paul was first introduced to the realities of war. He remembered vividly the aluminum wristbands they'd worn then. Name, rank and serial number and with the date the soldiers - their brothers - had gone MIA, missing in action - stamped in black letters onto the shining surface.

Paul's father shook his head. *How the hell can this timid boy, disinterested in the glories of battle, actually come from my loins?* he thought in dismay.

Inwardly, Paul felt sick and guiltily unpatriotic. All he'd ever seen of war was misery, heartache, and terror.

Towards the war's end, his friends often repeated, "I'm *so sick* of going to funerals."

Paul's father pushed him regardless towards a career in the military. Paul dared not push back. Instead, he'd applied for a scholarship in commercial illustration at the San Francisco Institute of Art, won it, and moved out.

Paul left his childhood home without fanfare or congratulatory back-slapping from his father.

Suitcase in hand, he'd looked back only once at the two silhouettes of his parents. His father, tall and rigid as an M1 rifle. His mother, short and slumped in abandonment. They stood three feet apart with the sun shining between them.

A Very Practical Solution

After graduation, Paul secured a part time job as a printer's assistant, rented a run-down apartment in the Castro district of San Francisco, and began eagerly to paint pieces for his portfolio.

Gregg's first sitting had simply been him posed in a chair while Paul scratched away, trying his best to capture Gregg's regality onto the canvas.

Over the months, Paul's art and Gregg's literature had embraced into an intertwined melody of seduction. Long nights and beautiful sunrises swept Paul into a giddy sort of bliss. They spoke of plans to travel to Europe. "You'll love it there," Gregg told him, "the sun setting on the Seine will simply *take your breath away!*"

Gregg glanced toward Paul's face as he spoke, seeing it awash in the stupid, frozen glow that could only be the telltale sign of love.

After a few months, it was just easier for Gregg to stay at Paul's apartment instead of taking a taxi back to the mansion. Overwhelmed in love, sprinkled in lust, Paul asked him to move in.

Paul stood against the wall, watching as the room filled with Gregg's entourage and sweaty, well-paid movers.

I had no idea he had so much stuff, Paul thought to himself, seeing boxes and trunks brought into the small apartment.

Gregg stood in the center, organizing it all with military precision. Shouting out where this or that goes, as Paul stood frozen, not in love but anxiety, watching the space, that only a few months before, had been exclusively his. Paul cringed as a mover bumped into the easel, almost crashing it to the floor.

Family had looked upon Gregg's move as "Two friends sharing a space. Very economical," they'd applauded, adding, "A very practical solution," to avoid thinking anything else.

Gregg's friends, young men the same age as Paul but from wealthier families, had eyed him with suspicion. *They probably think I'm a gold digger,* he thought to himself, *little do they know.*

Gregg had not, in the four months they'd dated, slid even one penny to help towards the expenses. He'd said, "Very soon Paul, the funds from my family," which Paul learned was the mother, "will come."

Gregg had no income himself. He'd told Paul, he was writing a novel. He rarely worked on it, not in front of Paul, anyway. He showed interest but had never seen it.

When questioning him, Gregg roared, "I must await the inspiration until it reveals itself to me!" Then he hinted, "It's going to be a fabulously scandalous book. One that will show everyone, from congressmen to rent boys, what really goes on in this town. I may have to publish it posthumously though," he giggled, "so I won't get a contract put out on me! It's bound to have the whole city in an uproar of gossip. *Absolutely everyone* will buy it, if only to secure they are not in it… *or to assure they are!* Oh! If only they knew what I know!"

It was true, Paul thought to himself, Gregg *really was* that famous. He'd never known anyone with such a full social schedule. From top restaurants to local clubs, lavish charity functions to formal embassy dinners, it was Gregg whom people looked for. Standing beside him ensured social success. "It's just because mother is so renowned," he'd said. "Her status in this city is famous!"

Somehow these flamboyant discussions had overrun any practical talk of costs, quickly dismissed by Gregg, who'd stated simply, "Writing is *my muse,* Paul, not for purchase like an old whore!"

Where did all these men come from, anyway? Paul wondered as he looked around the room.

He recognized some of them from that day on the Embarcadero. They hadn't warmed to him nor he to them.

Accompanying Gregg to parties, they dressed in the latest fashions and remained stolid toward Paul and his clothes. Gregg pooh-poohed their bitchy scorn but added, "Just try to get along, Paul. They don't mean anything by it," then added, "but *you could try* to dress a bit more fashionably, Paul. At least by not wearing those paint-splattered jeans. They are *colorful*, I'll give you that, but *really,* Paul."

Soon the crowd had switched off Paul's tiny transistor radio having somehow managed to install Gregg's huge speakers. Amid the crowd and the movers, the tune of *Chains of Love*, boomed into the air. The boys screamed in delight and began to dance, sliding up to the muscled movers who quickly squeezed from their embrace, escaping out the front door.

Gregg called out, "Well, boys, you've scared off my slaves! Time to break out the champagne!" A cork popped as a roar of celebration filled the room. Gregg held up his glass and said to the hushed crowd, "Here's to my new abode!" and they cheered again.

Paul scowled, thinking, *He didn't even say, "Here's to OUR new abode!"*

Gregg looked across the room at him and smiled.

Paul looked at him sheepishly and thought, *What the hell am I bitching about, anyway?* He scolded himself, *Tonight I have my lover, the love of my life here with me. I'll wake up to his smile and kiss him goodnight. Our nights will be filled with the delight of him reading lines from great novels and I painting his beautiful face. What more can I ask for?*

Yet deep inside, Paul felt a tingle rise in his belly. Not the butterflies of love, but more like a red flag waving.

Gregg leaned against the wall, arms folded, eyes overseeing his successful party. One of the boys joined him, leaned over, and said, "Come on Gregg, *really?* What do you see in this guy, anyway? I know he's an artist and all, but not even *a bohemian one.*"

Gregg watched as Paul attempted to squeeze through the crowd, dumping ashtrays, collecting empty glasses. Then he answered, "I'll put it this way, my dear. This suits me. Imagine… having a convenient local hotel, with no need to tip."

They grinned as Paul looked over and smiled.

Cracks in Paradise

"The house is silent as a tomb," Paul said aloud. After picking up abandoned clothes and washing dishes, he finally sat in front of his easel, lit a cigarette with fresh coffee steaming beside him. He thought, *I've never seen anyone dress and leave so quickly. Like a hysterical butterfly.*

Paul had returned from work at 5:30, his job done for the day. Quietly, he opened the bedroom door into a cave of darkness. He whispered, "Gregg? Are you awake?" The lump on the bed stirred, one eye opened and blinked.

"What time is it?" Gregg roughly answered.

"Five-thirty," he answered.

"Whaat? OH!" Covers thrown from the bed in dramatic hysterics.

Paul said, "Have you eaten anything today? You must eat."

"What? Oh, no - no time."

Paul had rarely seen Gregg eat. A bit of croissant at midday, a forkful between shrieks of laughter at a restaurant, nothing close to a full meal.

Paul watched as Gregg pulled clothes from the now overstuffed closet, trying on one color, then another, dropping each to the floor.

"Well?" Gregg asked, "What do you think?" his eyes on Paul's, turning from one side then the other in front of the mirror, modeling his choice of a blouse with crisp cuffs, its color pale lavender.

Paul said, "It's cold out today."

"Whaat?" cried Gregg, groaning impatiently, "I don't want *a weather report,* Paul, I want your enthusiasm… for my outfit. Really, Paul, can't you put your artistic talent to use in place of this motherly thing you do? It's very annoying."

But I'm right, Paul thought, *it is cold. He dresses like we live in the Mediterranean not chilly San Francisco.*

He doesn't even own a proper coat and has only one umbrella which he hates to carry, constantly leaving it at every restaurant in town. The waiters all fawn over him, fighting like the umbrella was a trophy to return to him. He'll coo and then in a rush of foreign tongues, cry out, "Oh! Benoise! Merci, mi amour! Oh! Franco, grazie! Ciao, Bella!" then forget it again.

Gregg looked again into the mirror as he applied touches of makeup and mascara. His piercing emerald eyes slid toward Paul's, then he said, "What a strange gay you are. It's a good thing you never chose to work in fashion… you haven't a speck of good taste in you."

Paul bit back a retort. *Better to just let it go, not start a fight I'll never win.* But he wondered, *Why do you pierce little knives into me? Take what I told you in confidence and then turn it on me like a weapon? I never do that to you.*

Gregg tapped his foot impatiently. *"Well?"*

Paul smiled, then said, "You look gorgeous, as always."

Gregg kissed him, European style on each cheek and dashed down the stairs.

"To another appointment," Paul muttered, and thought, *Either to some charity event of his mother's... "She does so much for charity. I simply must attend,"* Gregg would say. *Or to another literary meeting. "The boys need me there, to guide them, they know nothing, poor lambs."*

Paul couldn't remember which place Gregg left for as he waved goodbye. *It's gone on this way since, when? Oh, yeah,* he thought, *since the night I screwed up.*

Paul had never imagined he wanted a marriage. *After all*, he thought, *I watched my folks, married for years... and so unhappy. But* I am *happy,* he thought, *we both are.* In his state of bliss, he began to imagine how great a marriage, a true commitment to each other could be.

Paul looked at the portrait of Gregg in front of him. He'd painted a lot of these in the three years they'd been together. Grabbing sketches of him as he chatted in a restaurant or drawing him as he slept. These images now hung from every corner on every wall. Each side of his character, each slightly different, all painted with love.

In love, Paul mused, thinking again of that one night, while they lay in bed, drinking and talking. The night he'd enthusiastically broached the subject of marriage to Gregg.

In place of sparkly enthusiasm, his reply had been a peal of laughter.

"In case you haven't noticed, *I'm gay, Paul.*" Then, seeing he was serious, Gregg grew angry and snapped, "*I'm gay*! What on earth do I need a marriage for? Why would I want the headaches that straights have? All the paperwork, and tax forms and *babies* for Christ's sake?"

His enthusiasm stifled, Paul replied, "I… I didn't mean… I know it's not legal, but you know, a commitment… with a ring to show our dedication of love for each other…" Paul let his words fizzle into the air, turning his head away.

Gregg turned away too, as, with all conversations that displeased him, he quickly forgot this one. But inwardly he cringed, *Marriage? Please!*

He had always imagined himself a beautiful, young, wildly spirited stallion. He envisioned pacing the borders of the corral, wandering into the fold, to be fondled over, until curiosity got the best of him. Then he'd soon bolt away, galloping free again.

Gregg's reply had shocked him. Looking at the paintings Paul thought, *It was too soon… to ask, to try to ask. But I am, hopelessly in love. We both are.*

Then Paul admitted, *And yet,* he thought, looking up at the painting, *it is art I've always been devoted to.* He thought Gregg was devoted to his writing, to literature. But at parties, in restaurants, he'd seen another side of Gregg.

He watched while he spoke to his entourage, they, eager- eyed, hanging on his every word, as he plucked lines and strung them up like colorful party lights, to the cheers of his charmed circle.

Paul stood in disbelief as Gregg bowed to their cheers, knowing full well that none of them had a clue. The lines all came from famous authors and were not written by Gregg at all.

Other things had begun to irritate Paul as well. Every afternoon when he returned from work, he'd watch Gregg spring from under the covers he'd slept in all day, dress in a rush, then sprint out the door.

Paul mused, *Gregg's taste in fashion, what had in the beginning left me in awe at his ease with himself, seeming like a magical chameleon with a different look for every day. On days when leaving to the literature meetings, in cape and hat over his brow, the Oscar Wilde look. Or to parties, his metallic blazer shimmering, capturing his emerald eyes - changing his clothes sometimes four times a day. Fluttering like some hysterical butterfly,* he thought, *from one social gathering to the next.*

Which leaves me here, abandoned, alone. So many paintings surrounded him. *I painted to impress him, to show my love for him.*

Yet Paul was surprised to see that Gregg's ego seemed to have finally grown tired of looking at his own face.

He thought, *I've always painted what is in front of me. Unlike a writer or psychologist, I don't search for the reasons why people do as they do. I take people as they are: face, eyes, body – handsome or not, scarred, or lovely, body of Adonis or simple boy, these are whom I've painted.*

Paul was continually baffled when people spoke to him of his portraits, commenting, "Wow, this guy is evil!" or "I see this guy is up to no good," Paul mentally scratched his head at these comments while nodding in feigned agreement. He just couldn't see where these comments came from.

Paul dismissed the memories to ponder whom he would paint today. His mind flashed on a man - a long ago tryst at a local bar during his college days.

He'd been drinking for a while. After a few beers, he left in search of the toilet. While busily relieving himself, eyes front, he heard the door open. A man came up and stood beside him. Paul glanced into the mirror above the urinal, then glanced over at the man beside him, who's eyes were locked on his. He then backed into the stall and Paul followed.

Sweat poured over them, bathing their skin, drenching their clothes. They'd exploded together.

The man bore down on Paul's back, whose hands leaned flat on the dirty tiles to support the weight, uniting them as one panting beast.

The man peeled off him. He heard a zip of pants and a buckle fastening. Then the door opened, loud music and crowd noise floated in. All went silent again as the door closed behind him.

The canvas stood in the sunlight – bare and naked – intimidatingly erect before him. He thought, *maybe a new figure will be good for me to try*. He took the charcoal stick between his fingers and imagined a man's body before him. *All angles. Chin, torso, full and strong, confident, head high, defiant to whatever life throws at him. He is a boxer,* Paul imagined, *a fighter. A man who can take a punch and still stand.*

He sketched the lines quickly, fearful of the image escaping his eyes. He drew what was in his head: Images he'd seen in museums during his college days, posters from the 1930s.

Working men with strong muscles bulging in tight shirts, wet with sweat like a second skin, sleeves rolled up above the elbow. Chin and shoulder angles sharp against the circular forms of machinery, men in unison with industry, line against form.

As he worked, the rat-a-tat-tat of internal instruction ran through his head: *The black line, cut horizontally left to right – the shoulders. A slash diagonally from both shoulders, to form the triangle of chest.*

Flat lines there, left to right, just below where the nipples lay, flat dials, then below, just under the chest for the muscles there, one center line, straight down from neck to crotch. Branching out, smaller lines to form a six-pack stomach.

Paul felt the shimmering inside, a familiar rush rippled through him, as if fingers were stroking his belly, slipping down into his jeans. He was tempted to stop, to relieve the throbbing he felt below.

"Later," he murmured, stopping his fantasy, knowing this passion was better used for the painting, than release.

That tension, of sex or not, kept him working, his lust for sex driving the painting, the body on the canvas. *The viewer will feel it too,* he thought, *that longing.*

He drew the face in profile, a wavy line to form the lips, rounding slightly for the upper lip and beneath it, a fuller one. He paused to imagine biting it, then continued sketching sharp cheekbones, wide brow, flat nose and finally, the eyes of clear, baby blue.

Paul stood back from the painting and lit a cigarette. Squinting through the smoke, the rush that had gripped him had now eased. He was completely immersed in the work, with the man standing on canvas before him.

Paul turned his back from the canvas in search of a tube of azure blue. He'd not heard Gregg enter through the front door, who sashayed a little dance around the room, stopping suddenly in front of the painting. He gazed at the blue-eyed man, with muscles bulging inside his tight shirt. He was annoyingly beautiful.

"Who's this?" he asked tersely.

"Hmmm? Who's who? Paul answered, searching the palette for cadmium red.

"Him!" cried Gregg, stabbing toward the image.

"Who? Oh, he's no one…"

"No one? *What do you mean, no one?!*"

"I mean, it's a man out of my head, out of my imagination"

"No! I don't believe you! You couldn't have painted him so realistically if he'd not been standing in front of you."

Gregg stomped around the room shrieking, "Where is he? I didn't see anyone when I came up the stairs."

"That's because there is no one…I told you, he's from inside my head."

Gregg studied the painting then said tersely, "I don't believe you." Then, "Is he why you don't paint me anymore?"

Paul sighed and said, "I paint you all the time… look around … everywhere… it's you!"

Gregg looked at the images of himself, disturbingly realistic, his every mood, there, captured forever.

Paul thought, *You used to love being painted by me. Now, instead of seeing how I perfectly captured the regality of your profile in the evening light, you roar, "Darling! My nose cannot be that long, surely!"*

Gregg gasped, suddenly remembering the novel about a gorgeous young man, whose portrait and himself had remained innocent and young, while everyone around him became old. He'd sold his soul to the devil to stay young, but in the end, he'd crumpled, turning to dust.

Paul had captured his moods in exact, startling realism. At every turn, an image of himself stared. It had begun to unnerve him and though he'd never admit it, he resented Paul's talent as well.

Gregg stomped around the room, crying out, "Isn't there any mail?"

Paul tried to concentrate, but soon gave up. He answered, "Yes, Gregg," pointing to the table with his paintbrush, "It's there, right in front of you."

Gregg snatched the stack of mail, impatiently flipping through the pile, letting each float to the floor until exclaiming, "Ah *hah*!" grasping the letter he'd been searching for.

Pulling it out and ripping it open, he scanned the contents without interest, dropping each page to the floor. Then, holding the paper as if it were an Oscar nomination winner, he revealed the check. Triumphantly, he fanned his face with it and in sing-song staccato, he said, "At last, mother dear has come through… again."

Talking more to himself than Paul, he said "It's not as if I'm an expensive commodity," as he glided around the room, stating, "her monthly luncheon expenses add up to more than this!" He flicked the check viciously. "Ah, well, she has to keep a leash on me, the old… battle-ax!"

Gregg glared at Paul while dancing around the room, waving the check in a teasing, unplayful banter. Then, summoning forced bravado, he brightened and said, "Well, what's on today – champagne at Top of the Mark? Or no, that's mother's stomping ground, the old… dear."

He looked toward Paul, stopping in his tracks and said, "Or no, not today, right, Paul? Too busy working… again."

Getting no further reply, he turned on his toes and with his hand on the doorknob, he said, "I'm going out."

Paul wished he could just let Gregg's moods roll past him.

He pictured a train traveling at full speed with people on the platform, hair blown at crazy angles, leaning sideways. Their clothing blowing in a rushing force, leaving them haggard and bewildered, as if washed onto a beach after a tsunami.

Paul wished he could just get off at the next station and walk away.

He tried to go on, but Gregg's hissy fit had worked its poison. Glancing at the door as it closed, he noticed the forgotten cloak. Cursing, he threw down his brush, grabbed the cloak and his own dirty jacket. Opening the door, he shouted, "Gregg! Wait up!" Gregg stood at the top of the stairs, his foot tapping impatiently.

Paul softly said, "You - you forgot your cloak."

Gregg smiled, touched him on the cheek and said, "You really *do* care." Then, with renewed vigor, he said "So, where shall we go?" while marching down the stairs. Hearing no footfall behind him, he paused, still with back to him, he said, "Coming?" as Paul hurried after.

What had begun as a mostly comfortable, eventually non-sexual and now increasingly indifferent relationship had somehow become all about Gregg.

He'd grumble, "Why don't you paint me anymore? It's because I'm old and sagging, isn't it?" his emerald eyes flashing like a switchblade in challenge.

Paul put his brush down and softly replied, "No, of course not, Gregg, you're always beautiful." Lately, Paul replied more with fatigue than enthusiasm.

Gregg eyed him, as suspicion and relief crossed his features. Then, demurely, like a child asking for a toy in the window, he whined, "I'm bored!"

This, Paul knew by now, was said in challenge. He was baiting for a fight.

Gregg, not getting an answer quick enough, his claws out now, spat his words as a gauntlet between them. "You're *boring*, Paul. Getting nowhere, he turned and said, "I'm going out."

Gregg looked at Paul as someone who at first had been fun to play with but had become monotonous. Now, he was just a convenient companion to live with.

Gregg stood in the Hide Away bar on Mason Street, watching and waiting – never for very long – until a man approached him. If the man leaned toward him and whispered something amusing, he'd leave with him. Sometimes, only as far as the toilet or the alley behind the bar. If especially intrigued, he'd walk across the street to the park with him, glance up at the stars while commanding, "On your knees, boy."

Fear in the Air

It came on suddenly. At first, only as sluggishness but then becoming extreme fatigue. When Gregg no longer wanted to go out, Paul realized this was not in Gregg's character, not at all.

Paul kept at him, insisting that he go to a doctor or a clinic at least, to see why he felt so worn out. There'd been talk of a new disease that did not yet have a name. Gregg characteristically spent his energy ignoring then denying any information that displeased him.

Meanwhile, Paul pretended indifference to the dark foreboding forming in his chest that he'd not done enough, cared enough or even loved Gregg enough, or perhaps, at all. Work and caring for Gregg began to take their toll on him, who was himself exhausted. Against his better instincts, he stayed, as any good wife should.

The two men snapped at each other, becoming like animals trapped in a cage. Until one day, everything shattered.

Gregg glided around the room, looking more like a fairy in a 1930s musical than a man of intellect.

Stabbing his finger at Paul, he barked, "You're boring, Paul. You do nothing but mix colors all day long! And not *live* in the color. I want to live in the color, Paul, not just sit here, day after day, watching you mix color, the *same color, for Christ's sake.* How boring is that? Over and over again.

    Paul patiently explained that it was, "not the same color, but variations. The color was not yet perfect, it takes time and yes, perseverance to get just the right hue to express the tone of the scene. It's not like writing when you have a lot of scenes."

    Gregg only barked at him, "Red, rose, fuchsia, who the fuck cares? It's *red,* Paul, just paint it and get it over with! But no… you go on." With theatrical impatience, he rotated his arms at his side like a Ferris wheel, round and round, "on and on with the same damn color." Gregg slumped his body and hung there, mime-like, a drooping, wilted flower. Talking to the floor, he said, "Will it ever just… be done?" With this, he collapsed onto the couch, an arm over his eyes.

    Paul said nothing.

    Gregg rolled over, sighing dramatically and told him, "I'm tired, Paul, you wear me out. Damn you, I'm sick and you don't care, not at all. I'm probably dying and you don't even care about me," then he began softly to weep, or pretended to. Paul watched as Gregg rose and walked to the door. Though anger and guilt raged inside, he did not move to stop him.

Gregg walked from the apartment, heading north toward his favorite bar, The Alley Cat, on Mason Street. Inside, he'd been noticed but he quickly grew bored. He left and walked to The Balcony, a leather bar. The bare flesh wrapped in leather seemed succulent to him but quickly became too warm inside, surrounded by sweating bodies. He walked directly through the club, out the back door and into the alley.

The sky had begun to rain softly.

"Ahh…" he said aloud, "here it's cooler." He closed his eyes and raised his face up toward the sky. "Mmmm," he said aloud, "the wet feels *so good*."

When he opened his eyes, two men dressed in black leather were watching him and smoking. Gregg was curiously aroused.

He walked over to one of them and boldly asked for a cigarette. One man raised his eyebrows as the other put a cigarette into Gregg's mouth, lighting it with a snap of his shining Zippo lighter.

Gregg smoked as he playfully fingered the sharp points on his leather straps. He leaned toward Gregg and whispered into his ear. Gregg giggled as the other man moved up behind him, sliding his knee between Gregg's legs. "Mmmm." Gregg smiled as he sucked the cigarette. In challenge, Gregg exhaled into his face, then threw the cigarette on the ground. The man crushed it under his boot.

The men waited, one slapping a whip to his thigh impatiently. Rain was coming down hard now.

Gregg smiled, took the arm of one, then the other, and walked into the darkness of the alley.

Paul walked to the street, discreetly glancing up and down for Gregg. The construction workers smirked knowingly. Paul turned left and walked with purpose up the street. On the corner, he raised his face to the sun, a rare occurrence. The fog had finally lifted.

He walked slowly, sometimes eyeing men, more often not. He sought diversion, something else to look at or think about. His inspiration was at its lowest in years. He left the apartment more and more these days, not so much because he cared where Gregg went, but to sort out his own restlessness. *And just*, he mused, *well, all of it.*

Paul could find no words to define where they'd come to. He thought, *A roommate, that's what I have, what I've become. Why didn't I see this?* Paul asked. The answer rattled inside his head, then, *What do you ever see, really? Except the canvas, the paint.*

"An artist, huh? Ya know, you'll never be famous until you die, right?"

He'd heard that line all his life. He'd finally learned to reply, "Well, then I will be the exception!"

Paul had always been a loner. Now, when he meets a man, or more likely, a straight couple, he'd smile at their invitation of a drink, stating he was just, "Too busy." This line was always accepted. Even probing by the girl about his "single or married?" status could not be rung from him.

Paul watched them walk away; the man's arm draped over the girl's tiny shoulder. In possession, ownership, or love? Paul always wondered but could never quite tell.

When they were almost out of earshot, he'd hear them say, "Nice guy, that Paul. A little odd, but nice. Good artist, though."

"Yes!" the man would chime in, "a wonderful artist… not in a cool, bohemian way though…"

"No," the girl added, "not that way, but well, nice," they both agreed.

A loner, fun, not the life of the party, fun. No, not that way but nice. Paul heard those lines ring in his head all his life. Which was fine with him. Leaving more time for him to work. *Ah, yes*, he thought, *the all-important work.*

Paul was burning with humiliation at Gregg's words about his work. Words that Paul felt he always had to defend, to this man who didn't really seem to care.

Out of spite, Paul barked at him, "Not that you would know about art or writing at all. You, who haven't written a word since you moved in… only talked endlessly *about* writing with your bourgeois friends, mimicking Truman Capote and Tennessee William lines, complete with a Southern drawl. When have you even written a line after Uni?"

Gregg discarded the insult with a wave of his hand and said, "I'm bored," looking discreetly out of the corner of his eyes, "and lonely."

"Lonely?" he snapped, *"you?* With that brotherhood you troop around with, to all those literary meetings?" Gregg stopped in his tracks.

"Literary meetings?!" he said, giggling, "Is that where you think I've been?" then he broke into hysterical laughter, long and vicious.

Paul's face turned beet red. He felt like a hot poker had pierced his chest. Stuttering, he said, "That's… that's what you told me," His voice tapered off to a whisper, "I believed you."

Gregg stiffened, feeling attacked. Venomously, he spat, "Are you really *that naïve?* Yes, Paul, I've been out getting… *literary.*"

Paul said nothing in reply.

Of course, I didn't, he thought, angrily. *Just like when I was a boy and Dad came home drunk and started in on Mom, chastising her.* Paul saw this mother's face crumble in tears while neither she nor Paul said a word in defense. He sat frigid, seething in rage, wanting to smash his father's face in. Inside swirled a toxic cocktail of rage, fear, and finally, self-reproach.

Paul thought to himself, *How weird to think of that now, just when I was thinking of Gregg: my partner of three years, a man without integrity, that* Gregg *blamed me for his own betrayal.*

I was, Paul suddenly realized, *that naïve. Never did it occur to me that he was out cruising for sex. Is he the type for that? Yes,* he thought, *of course he is. To be surrounded by a cluster of boys at their master's feet, and himself the lecturer, a la Plato or Socrates, is a fantasy of Gregg's. One that he* obviously *tried to realize.*

Paul walked on, thoughts of shame and confusion inside. Attempting to justify the situation, he thought, *We've just rubbed each other the wrong way, lately. "Life is too short to hold onto anger about everything. Gregg always said that: Life is too short,"* Paul thought, *and now, God dammit, it was true.*

"Fucking disease! Why did he get this stupid disease anyway?" Paul shouted out loud, causing an old lady to rush across the street.

He became quiet and thought, *Where did this disease come from anyway? The news blames us gays. Hell, even that old actress, that orange juice lady, the actress I remember from when I was a kid - what's her name? Is saying that the disease is God's punishment of gays. What sort of insanity is that? This is* a disease. *It does not have a will of its own! Hell, even the President can't say the word GAY out loud. Some friend he is to his actor buddies. He just ignores it and hopes it will go away.*

This is a disease. *What the hell was wrong with everyone? Has society and the whole medical community suddenly gotten stupid? This disease is now turning the man I love, a man in the prime of his life, a man, who would - if he could ever just get some discipline - be an amazing writer. Who now, may never get the chance to see who he will be.*

Paul had heard the protests on the street, shouts of defiance floating up to his window. This whole cause had risen up, beneath him, leaving him feeling afraid, defeated, impotent, and mostly exhausted. *Yes,* he thought, *you go off and protest, I'll be here, cleaning the sick off Gregg's shirt.*

"God dammit!" Paul cursed aloud.

Lifeless, he paused to watch the fall leaves catch in a soft wind, rise up and off the ground, swirl in a tiny tornado movement, round and round, round and round, then settle again onto the pavement.

Paul kicked at them viciously, scattering them in all directions. Then chasing them, at first discreetly, then with abandon, as he'd done as a child. Catching the big ones under his shoes and crunching them, the sound releasing inside him what he'd not felt in years. Absolute joy.

He broke into laughter, stomping the leaves, thinking, *Crunch! Goes the face of my disappointed father. Crackle! Mom's sad, obedient face, crumpled.* Stomp! *The words of the couple; He's nice,* Stomp! *Nice guy!* Stomp! Stomp *that, Paul.* Stomp, stomp, stomp!

In the bliss of reckless abandon, Paul silenced all the negative voices from his life.

Pausing, his eye was drawn to a jeweler's window. Inside gems shone like beams in the sunlight. He noticed a Bvlgari men's watch: gold and elegant. Jangling the coins in his pocket, he felt his lack of income. His eyes moved toward silver necklaces, bracelets, and other stones. Then he froze. There, what he had seen on his father's brown and weathered finger, his whole life, a very simple gold ring.

He looked at the photograph beside it. The picture was of a pretty, young bride in a white gown and beside her, the groom, his broad shoulders straining in a tasteful, lined suit of light blue, reflecting his beautiful, clear blue eyes.

He looked at the gold ring on the man's strong hand, nestled within the tiny hand of a simple, pretty girl and thought, *I'll never have that, not ever.*

Paul became quiet, remembering what Gregg said to him before he left the apartment:

"I need to be out, in the life, experiencing all of it."

"All of what?" Paul asked quietly.

Gregg turned to him at the door and said, *"Just all of it, meeting fascinating men in all colors, having sex with them. Life is too short. My life, anyway, now."*

Gregg touched his cheek softly and said, "I know you love me and I'm grateful," then kissed him quickly, European style, on both cheeks and walked to the door, closing it softly behind him.

Paul thought, *If Gregg was really honest, he doesn't want this relationship either.* Walking slowly, he thought, *It's like a painting. It's done, but you don't want to leave it alone. You keep tinkering with it, putting in that one final stroke but then it all changes. Part of you wants to just rub it out, because the "great" painting you've just completed now looks all wrong. Changed and scarred forever. So, you walk away in disgust. "Leave it alone," you tell yourself. "Just walk away and have a cigarette and a glass of wine. Try not to think about it." Trying, as tempted as you are, not to just grab it, put it back on the easel, determined to keep trying.*

"Just walk away," he said aloud. *Yet,* he thought, *it must be completed, somehow.*

Returning home, Paul wiped his feet on the mat at his front door. He looked down to see a red leaf stuck to one shoe. Peeling it off, he studied it. The color was a beautiful deep, red, rich as a full burgundy wine and its subtle veins yellow brown, tracing the leaf's history. *Why is it,* he wondered, *that a tree never questions why it grows towards the light? It just grows.*

Paul heard a soft tap at his door. Upon opening it, he saw his neighbor, a lovely girl of seventeen from Guadalupe, her eyes tearful.

"Hi," Paul said to her. Then, seeing fear in her eyes, with concern, he asked, "Julia, what is it?"

She replied in a shaking voice, "Paulito," softly touching his arm, "Your friend, Gregg…"

"Yes?" he said, his chest tightening.

"He, a friend for him, came here to say Gregg is very, much more sick. He took him to the hospital."

Paul clasped her tiny hand in gratitude, in need of human contact.

Then he left her there on the stoop wringing her hands in worry, as he ran to hail a taxi.

The Farewell

Gregg lay in bed, his body exhausted. *I don't know myself this way,"* he thought. The white walls surrounded him. *What a bore this place is,* Gregg thought, *I've had the stamina of a teenager forever, but now...* He groaned. The fatigue had gotten so severe, he could no longer move. He closed his eyes and thought of the young men he'd loved. How he'd loved them. *So beautiful, so young. Life is too damn short.*

A nurse came through the door.

"How are you feeling, Gregg?" she asked him with a smile.

He could think of no sarcastic retort and said so.

She chuckled and said, "That's all right. Your mother is outside in the waiting room. Shall I send her in?"

"NO! I don't want her to see me this way!"

"Okay, Gregg, just rest now," and she closed the door.

He leaned back and closed his eyes, floating in a dreamlike fantasy.

He saw himself, only a few years ago. Seems so damn long ago... as he was then, pure, happy, and so damn young.

He was not the suave, hardened man he was now. *Of course not, not with this disease!* he thought.

Back then, his green eyes looked from under long bangs, fresh blonde, almost white hair with a shaggy cut to his shoulders.

Then there was James. We had been circling and watching, unsure if the sexual urge was mutual. But oh! What a sizzling current inside me every time I thought of him, pictured him, or saw him! Like a jolt of electricity up my spine and down through me and it showed. It was almost embarrassing! And yet, he thought, *it was so pure then. Everything was life! Sex! Joy! Out to the world, since June 28, 1969 - the Stonewall in Greenwich Village, New York.*

After that, everything was about how loudly we could shout, how brazenly we could kiss or clutch or embrace in public. The energy came from every quarter and oh! 1970 brought the pride parade down Polk Street, followed on the 28th by a "gay-in" in Golden Gate Park. What a sparkling, shining, glowing crowd of men and women. All of us, proud to say out loud who we love, who we are.

But across town, down Geary Street, was the Peace March of April 24, 1971. There were groups of men and women, not so happy. Yet, just as loud, proud and now with a fighting spirit to save themselves, their friends, their brothers, against the Vietnam war.

It was a subject James and I couldn't think about. We knew the draft notice would come any day. It was a terrifying piece of paper that could find you anywhere. And to not obey was to be thrown in jail. We all knew what happened to men in jail who were gay and unpatriotic. Things that the police looked the other way from, pretending not to see or care.

The difference between the gray-suited, black-tied and the colors of love, of freedom, of loving whom you wanted to, or to fight for your future, the right to have *a future, to not be shipped out of the country to Vietnam. These deep lines were drawn through the city and the nation.*

I wanted none of it. I'd pleaded with him to run away, to not go, to instead go to Canada, and I'd help him, somehow, even though my father was still alive and a conservative, black-suited banker. Pleading for my male lover was out of the question. James had graduated two years before me. I was still trapped at Uni.

He got the draft notice in May 1972.

We made love all night and into the next day. I could not go to the train, like all the other wives did, to watch him leave and wave goodbye.

I stood behind a pillar at the station, hoping he'd see me as his train left for the place he'd go for instruction in the Army.

We wrote to each other. I used the name Mary. Perfect for me, right? I had him write in care of a friend's address, so no questions were asked.

Then, he was shipped off to Vietnam. For a few months, I got letters. Until one day came a very official looking letter. It read, "I have been asked to inform you that your boyfriend, James, has been reported dead in… at… On behalf of the Secretary of Defense, I extend to you and your family my deepest sympathy in your great loss."

I still can't remember the dates, or where he'd been killed or who sent the letter to me. A friend of James, I guess. I must have blacked out. I know I went out and got drunk, which I rarely do, then I was violently sick. My parents thought I had the flu. They didn't know that by then my only thought was to die, to be with him.

Paul sat across from Gregg's mother, silently watching her, fascinated, as she fiddled with the diamond wedding ring between her aged, well-manicured fingers. Unconsciously turning it round and round, round and round. Light from the ceiling window catching, throwing colors like a lighthouse beacon across his eyes, as if to say, *"Never married. Never will. Not now, not ever."*

Paul never saw Gregg again. He'd asked the nurse to see him but was told, "Family members, only." Gregg succumbed to pneumonia the next day.

When he returned home, Paul found a letter inside a book on the table with his name on it. Gregg had never given it to him, but he opened it anyway. *Why not?* he thought. *Soon there will be nothing left of him here… except the paintings.*

It read: "I once had love, the love of my life. He was killed in Vietnam. I never got over it. So maybe this will help you now, when facing the death of your own, your one love. Know that I am who I am, because of the tragedy I had to face alone. And I never told a soul about it, until now."

He had written it in the perfect flamboyant script that only he could make, signed simply, "Gregg."

Within a week, the same movers that had moved Gregg in three years ago, had returned with a very efficient secretary, and had taken every trace of Gregg away.

In the weeks after, Paul watched as the neighborhood they'd shared together, became a constant flow, not of rainbows but protestors and funerals. *God*, he thought, *I'm so sick of going to funerals!*

In the end, there was no reason to stay. When offered a new job in Los Angeles, he jumped without joy at the chance. He, out of all of them, had been luckier.

"No pay, though."

"Huh?" Paul said, waking out of his nightmare.

"No pay, painting pictures. That's why I act. Well," said Brad, smiling sheepishly, "Hollywood's version of acting."

Paul smiled, relieved.

"What?" Brad asked him.

"Ah, nothing." Paul said. Holding up his near empty glass, he asked. "Another?"

Brad looked into Paul's rich, Mississippi river brown eyes, *like going home again,* he thought, then smiled, and nodding his head up and down, said, "Definitely" as Paul motioned for the bartender.

They walked home slowly, side by side, to Paul's apartment. At the front door, while putting the key into the lock, Paul paused and said, "It's funny."

"What is?" asked Brad, looking into his eyes.

Paul answered, "I didn't expect you to be like this."

Brad kissed him gently, sensually, then said, "Funny, I expected you to be exactly like this."

Brad hadn't awoken when Paul went to an appointment the next day. He'd left Brad in bed and gone for an early appointment.

He returned to see Brad still asleep, but apparently had awoken, washed, then changed into another T-shirt, *a white one, one of mine I see.* Smiling, *sleeps like a baby,* he thought, *but a beautiful one.*

He looked at his body, strong and muscular, a white T-shirt pulled tightly across his chest, thighs straining in tight, white jeans, his smooth, domed head and gold earring shining in the afternoon sunlight.

Entranced, without thinking, Paul reached for a pencil and pad. He began to draw: quick, loose lines, flowing and easy, capturing every detail of his lover.

The open window blew the Venetian blinds slightly, causing them to bang softly.

Brad opened his blue eyes, confused at first as to where he was, squinting in the afternoon light.

Focusing on Paul, he crossed his huge arms, muscles bulging, slowly grinned like a Cheshire Cat just out of sleep, and gazed at this lover.

"Always workin', huh? You new in town, sailor?" he said, patting the bed teasingly, giving him a playful wink.

"Just one more minute," Paul replied, "I think I've got it." With that, he closed the book, tossed it on the table and went toward the bed.

Days later, the painting was finished to perfection. Paul was ready, but nervous to present it at the meeting of his new boss and colleagues. He'd covered the piece with a light transparent paper to add to the flourish of the unveiling.

"This is," Paul said in a clear, strong voice, lifting the vellum paper to unveil the image, "Mr. Clean!"

The painting showed a huge chested man, arms crossed, muscles bulging in an impeccably clean, white T-shirt and work pants, head bald, tan and shining, a knowing wink smiling into their faces, and a gold ring in his ear.

A gasp rang out in unison. Paul tensed. Then an explosion of cheers flooded the room as they called out, "Great!" patting Paul's back, all smiles, with cheers of, "Well done, boy, great!" ringing in his ears. They hadn't even mentioned the earring.

The gold ring would stay.

This novelette is dedicated to all the wonderful Women's Bars, past, present, and future in every country on the planet.

Tattooed Chica

by Chantz Perkins

TATTOOED CHICA

By

CHANTZ PERKINS

<u>Tattooed Chica</u>

Bar Amour

The Red Chair

Silverlake

The Secret

Peg

The Search

Bar Amour

Peg Morton walked from her car up Santa Monica Boulevard, just past Little Frieda's coffee house, into the woman's bar. The cool darkness inside clashed with the bright sunlight she'd just left.

Squinting into the shade of the bar, she looked around.

A few women sat at a small, round table. They looked up at her briefly, then continued talking. Otherwise, the place was empty.

Opting for a seat at the bar, she pulled out a stool and sat down. Peg heard a wolf whistle directed at her.

Jamie the bartender, came out of the back room laughing.

"Nice, very nice," taking in Peg's fresh red lipstick, flowing apricot blouse, tight skirt, and low pump heels. She said, "That's what you wear *to work?*" as she crossed her arms, nodding approval. "Me like… a lot. You're just off work?" she said, sliding a square cocktail napkin, with printed black font spelling *Bar Amour* across it in front of her.

Peg laughed and said, "Hi, Jamie, thanks for the compliment. Yes, I came straight from work. How are you? she said, smiling into her eyes, feeling the warmth of their friendship."

"Fine, fine. Same old thing. What can I get you?"

"Well," replied Peg, "I'd like a Cosmopolitan today."

"Hard day huh?" asked Jamie.

"Yes!" she said, "Today's shipment of supplies just about broke my back. One of your lovely pink Cosmos, just what I need."

"Coming right up!" she said as she reached for the shaker.

Peg watched her scoop the ice, pour in the vodka, and as usual, make a show of it by pouring the vodka from a high stream into the shaker. Then cranberry juice. She covered the top and began to shake. She slid a cocktail glass off the rack where it hung upside down, placed it on the napkin then poured the pink liquid to the top. The finishing touch was a juicy slice of lime, perched on the rim.

Pointing to the lime, Peg said, "This looks like an old school bathing beauty crossing her legs on the edge of a pool, doesn't it?" looking up at her.

Jamie said, "Umm, okaaay. If you say so. You're the artist, not me."

"Mmmm, delicious!" she exclaimed.

Jamie smiled and turned toward her work.

Peg looked at the colored bottles behind the bar, around the room towards the women at the table, then toward the front door. She wondered why there were never any windows in American bars.

Probably, she surmised, *because passers-by would look in and point their fingers, scolding us for drinking instead of working.*

Peg turned toward the bar, listening to the music that had begun to play and closed her eyes.

A voice came from her left. She opened her eyes, looking toward the sound.

"I'm here" the silky voice came again, a melody of Spanish flowing through it.

Peg blinked into the sun flooding through the open door. She could see a silhouette sitting at the bar, framed in the sunlight of the open doorway. Peg shaded her eyes to the glare, holding her hand up. Then said, "I see only a silhouette with a voice," and laughed.

"I am your silhouette fantasy," the voice replied.

"Oooo, really?" said Peg, giggling. "How exciting. Come… *reveal yourself* to me." She watched as the figure moved from her left, walk slowly behind her, pull out a stool on her right, and sit down.

The woman was indeed Spanish, Peg thought, *and stunning. Her skin, smooth terracotta, long, silken black hair braided to her waist and dark chocolate almond eyes, lined in black like a raven's wing. Funky look too*, Peg thought, scanning her body, a tight, black T-shirt, black suspenders holding up loose khaki men's trousers and, on her feet, red Converse high top sneakers. Her rose lips smiled. "So… there you are," she said.

Peg laughed, smiling back at her then said, "I didn't see you sitting there."

"No," said the woman, "I snuck in while you were dreaming."

Jamie walked from the backroom and put a square napkin in front of her, smiling in greeting. The woman looked up and said, "Just a cold beer, any kind," then moved her eyes back to Peg.

Jamie poured a Budweiser from the tap into a frosty mug, placed it on the bar and then looked at Peg, smiling slightly while raising her eyebrows. Peg blushed, hoping the woman had not seen. She introduced herself as Ana Garcia.

"Nice to meet you Ana, I'm Peg Morton," she said, taking her hand and shaking it. The hand was long fingered, like a pianist, but soft and roughly textured. *She obviously works at a trade of some kind,* Peg thought in curiosity.

"So," Ana began, "how was your day?" as if they were old friends and for Peg it felt that way.

"Well, hard today," she replied, "but same as always."

"What do you do for work?" Ana asked her.

"Oh, I work in an office."

"Which one?" she asked, interested.

Peg paused. Ana thought she'd hesitated, seeming almost evasive. *Am I being too intrusive?* Ana wondered, then said, "If I'm not being too nosy."

Peg quickly answered, "It's an environmental company close to here, up on Robertson."

"That tall, dark, glass building?"

"Yes," Peg replied, "that's the one. And what do you do?" Peg asked her, wondering if her instincts about a trade were correct.

"I'm a landscaper," Ana replied.

"I'm jealous! How nice that you work all day in the sunshine!" Peg exclaimed, inwardly proud of her instinct about Ana's profession.

"Yes," Ana replied, "but not so nice on a hot day like this. It got up to ninety degrees today!"

"Very true," said Peg, relieved that the conversation had veered in another direction. Then, "I do appreciate the air-conditioning in my office on days like these."

They both sipped their drinks, then Peg looked at a silver necklace hanging around Ana's neck, and said, "Do you mind?"

She tenderly lifted it off Ana's chest with her fingers. It was a small figure of a woman, her robe deep blue enamel, her head bowed, with hands folded in prayer. Ana's face blushed from the rush of heat tingling up her spine at Peg's touch, as she asked her, "Is this the *Lady of Guadalupe?*"

Ana, impressed at Peg's use of *Lady,* not *Virgin* said, "Yes, most people think she is the Virgin Mary."

Peg had learned on her travels to Mexico, the Lady came from the actual sightings of the Lady of Guadelupe, long ago, by a poor, devout, indigenous Mexican peasant laborer. She said, "She's beautiful," looking up into Ana's eyes, who looked back.

Ana said, "So are you." Peg blushed, mumbling thanks.

Ana looked at her while she sipped her beer, thinking, *she's not exactly beautiful, not a typical blonde with a perky, little nose. Hers is a classical look, with features all nicely fitted together into a heart-shaped face, with long lashes over amber brown eyes and light blonde hair. Just over fifty,* Ana surmised, *but in great shape. There's softness about her as well, and almost a sadness, despite her animated personality.*

Ana glanced down at her watch and exclaimed, "I need to put more money in the meter. My Tattooed Chica is just outside. Are you staying? Do you want another drink?"

Peg asked her, "Tattooed Chica? What or whom is that?" and then said, "no, no thanks on the drink. I've not eaten yet, and well, these are a bit strong on an empty stomach."

"Then why not have dinner with me?" Ana replied enthusiastically.

Peg began to hesitate, thinking of all she needed to do tonight. Ana broke through her thoughts as if she could see them and said, "Come on, no work tonight. It's Friday! Have you ever had homemade chile rellenos?"

Peg perked up and said, "Mmm… Homemade? Really?"

"Of course!" Ana replied, "What sort of Latina do you think I am?"

"Well, then, yes, that would be great!" Peg replied enthusiastically, then she said, "but only if you tell me about the Tattooed Chica."

Ana asked Jamie for the bill, disregarding Peg's attempts to pay and guided her towards the door. Peg waved back toward Jamie and said, "Well, I guess I'm eating Mexican tonight."

Jamie laughed out loud as they left through the door.

Red Chair

Walking out into the softening sunlight, the day had not yet gone but the sky began to darken.

Women approached now in groups toward the door, some looking at Peg's skirt and heels, smiling their approval.

"Nice," she heard one of them say.

Peg turned and replied, "Why thank you." The woman nodded in return as Ana smiled, looking amused.

They walked up the street together, suddenly shy to be on their own. Ana stopped beside a convertible Chevy, beautifully renovated and highly polished, its chrome gleaming under the streetlights.

The color was a tint of blue Peg had never seen on a car before; painted like the deepest depths of the ocean, or the time of day just before complete darkness sets in, before the stars rise into the sky and grow bright, before the moon began demanding too much attention with her luminance. The car was this color, the best part of the day, blue twilight, a shade for lovers.

"This is *yours*?" Peg said, incredulous.

Ana's smile swept her face from ear to ear in pride. "Yep," she said, smoothing her hand over the polish, "This is *the Tattooed Chica*, this is my girl."

"She's a beauty! But why the name?" Peg questioned her enthusiastically.

Ana, beaming, said, "Later, at dinner," as she opened the door for Peg who slid onto the white bucket seat.

The chrome dashboard shone in the streetlights. In a row were a small AM radio, four small dials that showed gas and water levels, temperature and voltage and, in the center, a large dial showing the RPM, the speed. Surrounding Peg were spotless white leather doors and bucket seats, small open window wings and windows, rolled up; all were immaculate and polished with love.

The steering wheel was white as bones dried in the desert. At center was a ring of chrome, the horn, and onto the bone white surface was painted an intricate design of curling loops drawn into and away from each another as if a feminine hand had dipped a quill pen into gold ink and drawn it. Peg looked at it, then over to Ana's wrist, her hand raised on the steering wheel. Though tattooed in black ink, their designs were the same. *Hmmm… the Tattooed Chica,* thought Peg, *I like her… and her owner.*

"Want the top up?" Ana asked.

"No," Peg answered, "I want to feel the wind in my hair."

"Okay," Ana said, "but it can get pretty cold."

"Oh!" Peg's words tumbled in a rush, "How far away do you live? And what about my car? I know, you follow me to my street, it's just around the corner, on Havenhurst. Then I'll hop into yours. My car is parked just up the street."

Ana looked at her as she talked and thought, *Planning, planning, planning. This woman has to slow way down.*

Suddenly Ana's fingers were caressing Peg's neck, her soft lips gentle on hers. Peg felt an electric rush pumping through her veins and between her legs. *Oh, god*, she thought, *who **is** this woman*? as she opened the door and walked up the street with Ana cruising slowly beside her.

Peg arrived at her apartment, went quickly inside to drop her work bag, and thought to change her clothes, then decided against it. *Why not feel feminine tonight?* she thought to herself, glancing in the mirror and quickly grabbing a sweater on her way out.

She was on the front lawn as Ana pulled up. Peg raised her skirt playfully showing her a shapely thigh. Ana tooted the horn and called to her, "Hey sexy, want a lift?"

"Going my way?" she teased in reply.

"Sure, honey, any way you want to."

Peg smiled and hopped in the car. "Then let's go!" Peg shouted as Ana pulled the car from the curb.

They drove up Santa Monica Boulevard.

The engine roared with power when Ana revved it as she stopped at a red light. A car filled with teenage boys pulled up next to them, their music blasting some booming sound of no melody. One leaned out the window, shouting something to Peg, who then pointed to her ear, mouthing, "Can't hear you!"

He yelled louder, "Nice car, babe, is it fast?" while they too revved their engine in challenge. Ana looked straight ahead, her fingers tapping the wheel to the beat of her music. Only her raven lined eyes looked toward the right.

The light switched to green, Ana pushed the gas pedal to the floor, springing the car forward like a jaguar in chase. Within a minute, the car was left behind.

Looking back, Peg laughed at the shouting boys, their mouths each a small round "O," left in the distance in a cloud of disbelief. Peg watched the speed dial zip up to 60.

"WOW!" Peg cried, "She's *fast*!"

"You haven't seen anything," Ana shouted over the engine, "on the open highway, she soars!"

Peg threw her head back and yelled, "Yeee-haaaw!" as if she were riding a thoroughbred in full gallop through the desert.

Peg had never been a cowgirl, but tonight, on this blue stallion, she felt like one. She felt suddenly like a kid, her face glowing in excitement. Ana laughed at Peg's high spirits, watching her hair fly in the wind. She turned up the music and sat back, feeling… *terrific*.

They drove past Barnie's Beanery and the IHOP pancake house on the left, past Doheny Drive, La Cienega, and La Brea, crossing the Wilshire intersection, past the expensive district of Rodeo Drive and the Beverly Wilshire Hotel, through Hollywood, then finally, into Silverlake.

The district had a long history of artists. Writers Anais Nin and Raymond Chandler had lived here during their careers and now artists rented the homes, renovating them with fresh paint and glossy trim.

The homes were squat, square, wood structures with small green lawns, some with old cars set on cement blocks for repair. Most had large picture windows in front and small three- stepped stairs leading to a porch. Many had small artistic touches of colorful handmade wind chimes tinkling in the evening breeze.

Here the artists and gays shared the neighborhood with Latin families, creating a small community of pride and mutual respect, seeming to care more for beauty and working with love, than for money.

Ana pulled the car off the street, up onto two thin lanes of pavement. Patches of green grass between them served as a small driveway. The car rose up slightly as it came to a stop.

The house was small but lovingly cared for, painted a pale rose color with a front door of forest green. To the right on the lawn stood a huge banyan tree; its branches spreading out left and right like a Bayesian dancer; arms out and face in profile.

Covering the branches were green leaves and small red flowers that glowed in the rising moon like Christmas lights. The thick trunk was a twisting contortion of roots welded together and below, the roots bent and crooked as arthritic fingers grasping the dark, rich earth.

Attached to the house was a worn, wood front porch. On it stood two small, mint green, metal chairs, the sort seen in the Deep South, that were, on a hot day, cool to sit upon. They had a slight springy feel, a rocking motion created from the curved shape of the metal and the chair's simple design.

Peg looked to the left at a large picture window, where a white flowing curtain hung. A breeze blew it open and she caught sight of a poppy red, high-backed wing chair; the sort seen in expensive libraries or exclusive men's clubs of old.

The front door was framed by California morning glory, twisting through trestles to either side of the entrance on thin, green vines.

Peg stepped to the door as Ana reached in behind her, pressing her body close. Peg could feel Ana's breasts and flat stomach press against her back. Hot fire rushed through her, turning her legs to liquid, and making them weak. Ana leaned past her, put the key in the lock and opened it. Peg, her legs shaking from lack of food or want for sex, she wasn't sure, stepped into the house.

The room was small but cosy. The floor was caramel-colored hardwood, its history shining on it with cuts and gashes like an old face of character with wrinkles, gleaming in pride beneath the glossy varnish.

In a corner stood a small, arched fireplace, apparently still in use; she could smell traces of a recent fire with logs stacked to the side.

Beside that stood the red poppy chair with a small throw rug of mint green. Scattered around the room were dashes of color: small red or blue animals of hand painted, carved wood sat on shelves with books upright between them. A small archway led to the other rooms with walls of adobe, rounded at the corners.

On the whitewashed walls hung large black and white photographed images of women. Brown or black-toned luscious skin and only a round leg or the curve of hip shown through the tapestry that covered each of them. One showed a luscious leg peeking from the red poppy chair.

Ana came up beside her as Peg said, "These are beautiful." Then teasing, she added, "Your women?" Ana lifted one shoulder in a shrug as answer.

"You're the photographer, aren't you?" Peg asked.

"How did you know?" Ana replied.

"Well, beside the red chair," pointing to the right, "I can tell they're yours. They have an inner calm and spirit I can feel from you."

Ana smiled shyly then said, "Want a drink?" she asked, "or a glass of wine?"

"Mmmm… white wine, please, if you have it." Peg stood looking at the images of the women, all very beautiful. A memory of the kiss in the car under a twilight sky danced before her eyes, a wet tongue darting over her lips, pushing inside. Again, she felt the electricity swoon up her spine, pumping between her legs. *I won't be able to wait* she thought, as she walked over to the red chair, thinking, *yes, red is Ana's color, all right; passion and blood.* Putting all thoughts of well learned lessons of propriety and good manners aside, she kicked off her heels and slid into the chair. It was soft and warm, its arms embracing her like a lover.

Ana walked into the room and stood before her with two wine glasses in her hands, but her eyes were on the rise of Peg's skirt. She put the glasses on a side table and bent down, her hand touching a silky thigh, then into the darkness beneath her skirt.

Peg moaned softly. Ana leaned down, kissing her softly on the lips as Peg reached up to put her lips tightly onto hers, her hand behind Ana's neck, her tiny medallion necklace hung down, tickling the skin between her breasts.

Ana knelt in front of her, kissing her while opening her legs, reaching her hands under her ass, slowly pulling off her string. Ana paused looking at her; Peg's legs now open and wanting. She ran her tongue up one thigh and then the other as her hands caressed them, pushing them further apart.

Peg felt Ana's breath on her, moving down her body. Peg reached up, stretching her back, her hands grasping the wings of the big red chair, stretching toward Ana's tongue, now thrust inside her, into her dark place, a pool to dive into, a warm, sweet place.

Pleasure rose up from her as a moan of need escaped, as if from very far away.

Silverlake

The two lovers lay on their backs under the banyan tree, their dinner forgotten, cooling their heated bodies in the night air.

Ana's head propped in her hand, looked down at Peg, while tracing her finger along her loosened blouse. She said, "You were going to tell me why you named your car, *Tattooed Chica*, remember?"

"Ahh," Ana said, rolling over onto her back, looking through the branches, as the stars brightened in the deep blue sky. "Sure you don't want dinner first? It's kind of a long story."

Peg replied enthusiastically, "First the story, then dinner, then… I want to see your bedroom."

Ana raised her eyebrows at the thought.

Peg said, "I'd love to stay the night, if that's not being too presumptuous."

Ana smiled, showing Peg she'd hoped this would be the night and possibly weekend plan. She began her story…

"Mmmm, okay, if you need to hear this now… *Tattooed Chica* is a symbol for me - a sort of *metaphor*. Ana continued, "I grew up with parents of mixed cultures; my mother had come here from Guadalupe, Mexico to work in the fields, way back in 1950.

"My father, who was white, came from an upper-middle class family, whose roots extended way back in San Diego. The two met each other while he was teaching at a grade school. She had a job sweeping the floors of that same school.

"They began at first with only pleasant conversation, then he said to her, 'I'd rather see you grading papers instead of sweeping them up.'

"He encouraged her to study towards a teaching degree which was awarded not long after. She spoke his language in more ways than one, blossoming into a love affair, finally marrying a few years later. They had a son, then, several years later, a daughter, me."

Peg rose up on her elbow to look at Ana as she spoke. She could see in her eyes the picture of a mixed marriage in the 1950s and how difficult it could have been.

Ana continued, "Mama's brother, my uncle, had come to Los Angeles in 1940. He was not treated so well. His skin is deep brown like mine, so his sympathies leaned towards his Latin roots. For a time, he fell in with group of young men, roaming the streets of downtown L.A., spending his time shooting dice, frequenting the bars and looking for women.

Mostly though, he was a good guy and didn't get into trouble. But then came the Zootsuit Riots. You've heard of those, right?" She looked toward Peg for confirmation.

Peg nodded yes, while images came into her mind, what her father had told her about that time: *Summer, 1943, World War II in full swing. Trains pulled into Union Station in downtown Los Angeles, filled with servicemen, their pockets bulging with cash, taking to the streets, looking for drink in the bars, women to dance with, and maybe, if they got lucky, a bit more.*

Dad said the locals resented these soldiers coming into their territory, spending cash so freely in the bars, competing with them for the women. According to his story, the Mexicans began rolling - mugging the men, leaving them broken from blows to their heads and their pockets empty. Fights broke out, local police and MPs could only contain the fighting in spurts and were siding with the servicemen. Over a period of days, then weeks, the soldiers continued to flood downtown, and the fighting continued.

When the President heard about the rioting in L.A., citing it "Was bad for the moral of the service personnel," Dad said that orders came down the chain of command, "To just solve the problem, any way you can." A purposely cryptic message, interpreted by Dad to mean, "Beat the hell out of anyone who messed with them, no questions asked. Military personnel had stormed downtown in packs, beating up brown-skinned men at random. By then, the newspapers had sided with the military; their motivations regarded as honorable or at least, justified, since they were fighting in the war.

 Peg had listened to the story her father told. Its brutality and injustice causing her to inwardly squirm as she tried to justify it, realizing in that era, life was different, more brutal, and more unjust.

 She hoped things were different and society now, in 2013, was more lawful to Latinos but also to servicemen. She'd seen herself how soldiers had actually been spat on by protestors during the Vietnam War. Peg now flushed at the memory of her Marine father's words, knowing she was about to hear, for the first time in her life, the other side of the story.

 Ana continued, "Some of the Mexican men wore a costume, a sort of uniform created by the dancers of their Spanish roots: wide- legged black or striped baggy pants held up with suspenders, white shirts with full sleeves and tight cuffs. And a wide-brimmed hat and shiny, black, point-tipped shoes. You've seen them, right?" Ana asked Peg, who nodded confirmation.

 Continuing, Ana said, "Since the clothing was easily recognized on the street, they'd been targeted by the soldiers as well as any brown-skinned man or woman, they were swept up in a rioting frenzy. Some were badly beaten and thrown into paddy wagons, held for hours or days without bail.

"My uncle was unjustly targeted, beaten and thrown in jail. Our family had no idea where he was for days. I learned about this all years later. For a time, it had been a secret never spoken of. In the end, the city officials outlawed the zootsuits, sighting the waste of cloth during wartime. So that ended the zootsuits and with it, a strong part of Latin culture."

Ana seemed wistful, saddened by the telling of the story. Peg reached out to her hand and gripped it, running her fingers over Ana's tattooed wrist while thinking, *My history is so different than yours.*

Peg was silent. Then, bracing herself, she said, "Okay. The story you just told me? Well, my father was in the Marines in World War II. He told me about that time, because he was there, in L.A. downtown… on the other side… as a serviceman."

Ana seemed to tense, but just listened.

"When you told me that story, I thought, maybe my dad was one of the guys who beat up your uncle… I have no idea… but yes, he said he beat up some guys…"

They lay there; the air had suddenly become hard to breathe.

Defensively, for no other reason, Peg said, "He was a good guy though, he just lived at the time of... well, you know."

Ana stretched her back as Peg bent down to kiss her, then asked, "Your uncle, was he bitter?"

"Yes," Ana replied, "I learned much later that he was for years. But now he's living in San Francisco, married with kids of his own. His children have softened his scars and helped him to move on."

"You've given this a lot of thought," Peg said sympathetically.

Ana turned onto her back again and said, "I don't judge that time, no matter what the injustice. I can't imagine what it would have been like to be in a war, fighting and perhaps seeing your friends killed. Then coming on leave into this city, pumped up on testosterone, wanting only to get drunk and fuck, to forget all that you've seen. To grab for two days all that you'd been denied.

Although I have no testosterone myself," she smiled into Peg's eyes, "I can understand the fucking part but not the fighting. I'm more lover than fighter."

Her eyes softened, as Peg smiled down at her, replying, "Mmmm… you certainly are a lover."

Ana replied, "*You* are the lover, *an impatient* one," nodding to the red chair in the window. Peg blushed, her spine shimmering in pleasure. Then she said, "But you haven't explained about the *Tattooed Chica.*"

Ana laughed, "Oh, yeah, that's how this whole story started. Sure you're not bored?"

"Of course not," Peg said earnestly.

Ana went on, "Well, the tattoo part is a promise I made to myself long ago when I was a kid; to brand myself with my own Latina roots and those zootsuiters in honor of my uncle. I wear their clothing, as you can see."

Peg looked down at her body, her loose-fitting men's trousers held up with suspenders but with a tight, black T-shirt and red Converse high tops. Peg looked her over and said, "Mmmm, yes, I can see it, modernized of course."

"Well, yeah, a gal has to keep up with the times," she laughed, then continued, "so, the clothes don't explain the tattoo. I cultivated a zootsuit look the same time I'd by then realized I was a budding dyke, who loved women and was interested in 'guy things,' one of them being fast gorgeous cars. I saw this one," nodding toward the Chevy in the driveway, "and the design on its steering wheel became my metaphor. I had it tattooed here," turning her wrist, "a branding of my brown skin as a modern Latina woman, choosing to defy the standard of Latina women who married, stayed home and raised kids.

"The zootsuiter men had women who also dressed in similar clothes, not in dresses but in pants. Very rare for those days, and they were tough chicas too. Some even chose women to sleep with. They were not *'out'* as gay but were accepted as a different sort of woman.

"And the chica part, well, that means girl. *That* was the word shouted at me on the street. Me, a shy, frightened, little girl, hearing, "Hey Chica!" from men as they whistled and snapped their fingers at me. I swore then, that one day I would take that word as my own and make it stand for a different kind of woman, the woman I was trying to become. Now, before I starve to death, let's eat!"

They lay in the comfort of Ana's big bed. Its warmth came from their bodies intertwined, legs wrapped around each other.

Ana said, "Now that we've eaten, it's your turn to tell me your family history."

"Hmmm," Peg began, "I'm not sure if I want to tell you…"

"*What!?*" Ana replied, "a sordid past? So young?"

"Yes, that's another point" Peg said, "I'm not so young…"

"I know that," Ana said, "maybe a few years older than my age of forty-five…?"

"Well," Peg relied, "that makes me feel better… yes, about ten years older to be exact…"

Ana dismissed the comment as silly.

After a big inhale of air, Peg began to talk about her family. Her grandparents had come here from Chicago in the 1920s. Her only brother was married with two kids, living in Playa del Rey. Both her parents had been killed in a car accident several years ago.

Ana held her closer, not knowing what to say except, "I'm so sorry."

"There's more," Peg said, "but not tonight."

Ana held her as they both drifted off to sleep.

The sun shown in on their bed, and they both arose late, caressing each other, then Peg said, "I'm starving!"

Ana rose and went to the closet, taking out a training suit to slip into. She found a kimono for Peg, who held it up and asked, seductively, "A friend's?"

Ana slapped her on the ass and left her to scavenge through the refrigerator. Peg trotted after her on tiptoe and looking over her shoulder said, "Pleeease, coffee first - major priority for me - and please don't say that you have none."

Ana, sounding offended, turned to her and said, "Of course I have coffee! You go in the big chair and curl up. I'll make huevos rancheros."

"Yum! I've died and gone to heaven," Peg replied as she tiptoed into the den, curling up in the red chair. Remembering what had happened here the night before made her swoon.

After brunch, they walked around the neighborhood while Ana told her about the improvements to the area and its history, pointing out the funky cafés and art studios.

As the day crossed into early evening, they went into a Mexican bar for a drink. Ana walked to the bar and ordered in Spanish. Peg sat down, reprimanding herself for never having learned the language.

Ana brought two margaritas to the table: frosty and the color of sunshine with salt on the rim and a fresh lime.

"They look delicious." Peg held up her glass to toast.

Ana raised hers and said, "Salutas, mi bonita."

She clicked her glass to Peg's, who said, "I understood the first part, but the 'mi bonita'? What does that mean?"

Ana said, "It means, 'My pretty.' You *really* never learned Spanish in school?"

Pam blushed in shame and said, "No, I had a dream to be a painter in Paris, so studied French, though I can't speak that now either," and laughed.

They sipped their drinks, then Ana said, "So tell me more about yourself."

Peg sat back and began, "Most people think I'm crazy and that I live in the past, hell, maybe I do. I love this city, with its old Art Deco buildings downtown, the weird 1950 Jetson cartoon- style coffee shops, even the restaurants with 'Bob's Big Boy' standing in front. I've always loved it here. But from very young, I've had this *craving* to go to Europe. To see the architecture, the art, the cities where my ancestors came from."

"Where was that?" Ana asked.

Peg replied, "On my mom's side - Italian and Jewish, from the south of Italy, and on my father's side, Ireland. You see? I have drinkers on both sides," and laughed.

Ana chuckled, then said, "So, you traveled there - to Europe and...?"

"Um, yes," she said.

Ana pondered, *and again, a hesitation in her voice, like last night in the bar. As if to change the subject*, Ana noted.

Peg continued, "I've always felt that we are only a *part* of those who came before us. Like, what are we if not able to reflect on the past and learn from it? Isn't each breath we draw only because of the one we drew before it?" Then seeing Ana's confused face, she said, "I'm just crazy, that's all," and took another sip.

Ana said, "No! I agree completely. I feel the same."

"You do?"

Ana nodded confirmation, then said, "Go on."

"Well, in my opinion, so was it with history; all who came before us became part of our history, seeped into our DNA or culture, and that is who we are."

"And your family?" Ana asked her, "They feel similar to you?"

"Yes," Peg said, affirmatively. "I was brought up appreciating the craftsmen and women. To see something carved by hand, a sculpture, a chair, even a picture frame, to respect the work and love what went into making it. That's what I love about *your* house. All the art, the love, and care that went into everything,"

Ana sipped and nodded. "Mmmm, you see? We're very kindred in that respect."

Peg smiled as she looked into Ana's dark eyes, then continued her story. She grew up in a suburb near Santa Monica. Her mother scavenged the odd shops for furniture, often refinishing pieces herself. She had a love of art and music, a passion her father also had.

Peg's own studies of painting at city college, working odd jobs, then moving to Europe to be a painter. Her life up until now.

They walked slowly back to Ana's house, remarking on the sky, the places they saw along the way.

Entering the door, they held each other, savoring the moment. One by one, they removed each other's clothes, slowly, relishing the potency of their time together.

In bed, they made love slowly, carefully touching each other's bodies, caressing skin, lips, and shoulders. Then, when all passion was depleted, they slept in each other's arms.

The Secret

The sun shone through the blinds on this Sunday morning. Peg looked up at the ceiling, preparing herself for the talk she decided she needed to have. Beside her slept Ana. She looked down at her and thought, *Mi bonita, how will I ever say goodbye to you?*

Ana opened her eyes, blinking into the sunlight that came through the window.

"Hi," she said, wrapping her arms around her, stretching like a cat.

Peg, her courage wavering, said, "Hi," her heart breaking. Ana looked at her, concern darkening her brow.

She said, "What's up?"

Peg now turned toward her and said, "There's something I haven't told you."

Ana sat up, sensing the coming words may not be those she wanted to hear. She braced herself then said, "Go on."

Peg got up and began pacing the room, then said, "I told you I was born here."

Ana nodded.

Peg went on, "Well, it's like this. I have to go back to Europe."

Ana jolted, then said, "Okaaay… when?"

Peg replied, "On Wednesday."

Ana's body was now straight up and rigid. She said, "For how long?"

"For always," Peg replied, then, "at least until next year."

"But," Ana stuttered, "your job, your apartment," purposely leaving out the word, "*us*."

Peg stood before her, her head raised in defiance, "The thing is, I'm no longer a U.S. citizen."

The words spun in her head. Ana thought she'd not heard correctly. "What do you mean, *no longer* a citizen? You were born here!" she exclaimed, staring at her, baffled.

Peg said, "I renounced my U.S. citizenship several years ago."

"*Renounced?* As in *gave it up*? But why? How? Who made you do that?"

Peg sat on the bed, the hated explanation she'd given so often she now repeated again, almost as if she were an automaton, reciting someone else's words.

"I was working as an artist in Europe, I told you that."

Ana nodded, fear and anger rising inside her. She now also paced the room, clenching her fists.

Peg said, "All went okay, very good in fact, especially in London, my work was selling really well there." She smiled at Ana, who tried but failed to show enthusiasm. Peg had seen the reaction she'd gotten from other Americans, but continued talking anyway, without really knowing why.

She said, "With a U.S. passport, I could only stay in London for six months at a time. So, I traveled back and forth, painting the work in Amsterdam and delivering it to London. That went well for a few years. Then, in 2008, the banks failed, and the London bankers - well you must have seen it - they were no longer awarded large bonuses paid to them, so people could no longer buy, or invest in art, not like it had been: the art market dropped by seventy percent!"

Ana said, "That's a lot!" then slumped again into fear, still trying to brace herself for the outcome of this all.

Peg said, "Yes, it was. I know a lot of people lost so much more, but for me, it was my career, a dream I had fought for all my life. And suddenly, it became the beginning of the end."

Ana said, "That's when you... *gave up?*"

Peg stiffened at that term. She'd always prided herself as a fighter, able to pull up her bootstraps and keep going, no matter what. Defensively, she said, "*I didn't give up.* I chose something, the best decision I could make at the time. I moved back to Amsterdam full time, turned my back on art and looked for work. My artist dream was no longer sustainable anyway, and just before that, both of my parents had died in a car crash."

Ana knew about her parents. Peg had tearfully told her the night before. She remembered feeling so proud of her, how bravely she'd spoken of it and feeling a love for her that was overwhelming.

Peg went on. "Faced with this all, I realized that I no longer had anyone in America really. Except my brother who had a family of his own. And besides, the waiting list to apply, for someone dependent on a sibling, is *twelve years*.

"After ten years of debate with myself, I went into the U.S. Consulate and told them I wanted a European passport, which meant I had to renounce my U.S. citizenship. Again, I was told the consequences, but this time, I went ahead and signed the papers, crying all the while. It was horrible."

Ana said, "But why? Is that an American rule?"

"No," Peg replied, "it's Dutch. You can't have dual citizenship unless it's from marriage. The U.S. doesn't ask you to renounce unless you ask for citizenship in another country, where you can live forever with a permanent residency card."

"Couldn't you have done that in Amsterdam?"

"A reasonable question," Peg said, "I did have a permanent residency card in Amsterdam for years, but

London immigration couldn't read it. It was written in Dutch."

"They'd always toss it aside, then ask to see my U.S. passport. Each time they stamped it, completely haphazardly, not organized at all. They saw I was traveling back and forth many times, too often for their taste. They finally told me, *threatened* me really, that they suspected me of living there. If they found that to be true, I would be deported and never let back in! All my artwork would have been confiscated, my bank account frozen, my gallery connections severed. Each time they accused me of trying to live there, I got more and more desperate."

The room was silent now, as if a lethal poison floated in the air.

Ana paced the room and said, "It's such a huge thing though, was there really no other way? Can't you apply here with your work? Get a green card? GOD! I *can't believe* I'm having this conversation *with you!* The sort of talk I've had with my South American friends, but *YOU?* You were born here and you… you just gave it away."

Peg looked her straight in the eyes and said, "What a little pal you are."

Ana, red-faced, said nothing.

Peg was livid now, mostly at herself. She said, "I'd put it off for ten years! I tried every other possibility. The lawyers I saw all told me to marry a Dutch guy, since marriage was accepted but gay marriage was not.

"Even then I didn't have anyone to marry, and it *pissed me off* that my worth as an artist was nothing to the government there - or here, for that matter. Marriage is considered the only value in this world, marriage or money. All *solo, single artists are left to fend for themselves!*

"And no, to your question, I can't apply here based on my work. I have a volunteer temp job."

Peg was putting on her clothes now, then said, "But you know what? In the end, it was the only thing I felt I could choose at the time. My money was running out and the art, well, that was all for nothing. A twenty-year career died as a crumpled dream. It's a choice that I tear myself up about on a minute to minute basis. It's fucking ironic though, isn't it? My ancestors came here to have a better life, free of oppression and two generations later, I go to Europe to do the same. To be a lesbian artist in Europe, to not accept society here as it was. Instead, I tried to find a place that would accept me, fighting for my dream as a woman artist.

"Well, that dream died with the bank crash. And who knew things here socially and politically would ever become so accepting? Gay marriage? *I never* would have believed it. Not in a million years! I know straight women, people who've been married two, sometimes three times. I look into their cupboards and it's like a scene from a spy movie: an assortment of colorful passports: red, brown and of course, blue, the U.S. passport. It makes me so angry! It's so unfair! *That I must marry to be considered a legitimate citizen.* But my art career counts for nothing at all!"

Tears streamed down her face as she said, "But dammit, it's done now and there's no turning back. I'm sick of beating myself up about this and having *you,* an *American citizen,* looking at me like I'm a terrorist or a traitor."

Peg had put on her clothes and was now searching for her purse. In finality, she said, "I'm going now."

Ana said, "I'll drive you."

"No," dismissing her offer, Peg said, "I'll call a taxi."

Peg punched in the number and moved toward the door.

The taxi pulled up on the street. Walking to the door, Peg softened and said, "Well, it's been wonderful… except this last part. If you want to get together before I leave?" she asked hopefully, then, seeing Ana's face said, "Well, goodbye then."

Peg walked to the taxi, got in and told the driver her address. She looked out the window, holding her hand up as a half wave toward Ana who stood in the doorway of the front door. Ana began to raise her hand but instead slowly closed the door as the taxi pulled from the curb.

The driver's voice said to her, "Señorita, mujer, you okay?"

Peg looked up at the rear-view mirror, his eyes on hers. Pain flooded through her as his accent and dark eyes reminded her of Ana.

She said, "Yes, I'm okay," and she looked out the window at Silverlake, disappearing from her view.

Peg

The taxi dropped Peg at her apartment. She walked inside and stood there, feeling like she'd just crawled out from under a bus she'd been thrown under. She thought, *Well, I can cry, but that never does any good.*

Ana arrived at her mama's house, a small bungalow in Culver City. Opening the screen door that always remained unlocked, she walked inside and put the groceries she'd brought on a wooden table. She looked around the joy-filled room and its gleaming surfaces, spotless as usual.

Her mama was always busy with redecorating, even on her limited teaching salary. She was forever making new bright things for her home with her hands. That was why her grade school pupils loved her so much, forever curious, joyful and young.

Ana stood, doing or saying nothing until she heard a sing- song Spanish voice call to her. "Ana, is that you?"

"Yes, Mama," she said, trying to sound more positive than she felt.

Peg remembered that day so vividly. She often could not sleep from the memory of it. The day she'd walked into the American Consulate office in Amsterdam. There, she met with the Consulate officer. He'd told her of the ramifications of what she was about to do: renounce her American citizenship.

She asked him, "I know there is now gay marriage here, but is it also legal in America? He shook his head, no. She thought, *So okay, that's it*. Then she told him, "I'll go ahead with the renunciation."

Still, he delayed her by asking, "There is a young woman before you, do you mind waiting?"

Peg shook her head no. She watched as the young woman, no more than nineteen, Peg decided, listened to the Consulate officer as he asked her questions. Beside the girl was a man, whom, Peg determined, was her father. She saw the worry scratched on his face, atop so strong a body, he seemed childlike as he watched, eyes wide and round with fear, his mouth silent. There was nothing he could do.

The Consulate officer listened to her story: something about her going to university and how she'd decided it was better to renounce. Peg hadn't understood exactly why - it made little sense to her.

As she watched, she looked up at a picture of the current U.S. President, then at her and thought, *Girl, don't do this! You're too young, you can't see now what may come onto your path. Just wait, you don't need to do this now.*

In the end, however, she had not. Peg felt a rush of relief. Almost as if it had been she, herself, that was saved, not this young woman she didn't know.

The Consulate officer came over to her and said, "Powerful, isn't it?"

"Yes," Peg replied and nothing more.

He looked at her with empathy, then said, "I'd like you to take this document and go outside and read it again and think about it. Will you do that?"

She knew she was purposely being delayed. After battling with herself for ten years, then finally steeling herself to come here, determined to get it over with, she felt angry with him. But in the end, she agreed.

Peg sat outside the American Consulate and lit a cigarette. Taking the smoke deep into her lungs, she held it there, remembering the time she'd come here after the 9/11 attacks on the Twin Towers. She'd brought flowers in memorial and signed the book of remembrance, writing the simple words, *Never Again*.

She exhaled with a sigh.

She thought of the young woman and her father. A father so much like her own. *He would have done that,* she thought, *he would have been racked with worry that I was making a mistake.*

He'd reminded her of the last time she'd seen her father, when she'd boarded the train from San Diego, going to Union Station in L.A., then flying back to Europe. The last time before he'd been killed.

He understood me so well, she remembered, *my absolute passion to be an artist, to go off into the world, to shape a career, put my mark in this world. We had a vocabulary of art shared only with each other.*

He too, had studied art. After World War II ended, he'd used the G.I. Bill to enroll at a university in Oregon. He graduated, then moved back to L.A. and married Mom. He'd gone from Uni into teaching at Chouinard Art Institute, then eventually, into television, the new creative venue using art as a new form.

He'd succeeded but knew only too well how difficult it was. How difficult it had been for me, to crack that glass ceiling overly crowded with men. But a woman? Not easy, not here. This, he knew.

So, when I told my folks I was moving to Europe, to "make it," he knew just how much that meant to me.

Peg sat, remembering him as he'd been on that last day. He stood with a puzzled smile, trying to look brave. She walked up the stairs inside the train. Looking down, she saw him on the platform, anxiously waving, looking for her through the dirty windows.

She'd waved back, smiling. *But he didn't see me,* she thought as a ping came into her heart, so deep, so pain-filled, she felt nothing until the forgotten cigarette had burned down to her fingertips.

"Damn it!" she cursed and put it out.

She now felt the tears that had, unnoticed by her, streamed down her face. She sighed, wiping them away, then looked down at the document the Consulate officer had handed her. And for the umpteenth time, she thought again, *Is this really necessary?*

Peg remembered the immigration authorities in London. How long they questioned her the last time she'd been there. The Spanish Inquisition entered her mind.

London, practically her second home by then, complete with partner, studio, her art, and the gallery she'd finally secured to sell her work, all waiting for her return.

The London authorities accused me of living there. That was after 9/11. So much inquiry and paranoia, so many questions, so damn much suspicion. They could turn me away and send me back to Amsterdam, never allowing me to return to London, freezing my bank account, confiscating my artwork. That was happening there every day.

Yet Peg knew it was only that woman, her partner at the time, who comprehended exactly what she herself had gone through. She, though highly educated in Bulgaria, was only offered the jobs of immigrants.

She'd lived what it felt like to be considered *nothing better than* an immigrant. What it meant to leave her country, so she could be whom she truly was, a gay woman, and what it meant to find the life she couldn't have in her own country. *Yes, we experienced that together. It gave us a bond, but not one strong enough to endure the political fallout.*

And, also, I would have had to start over.

The years I'd built up in Europe didn't count in Britain at all. I'd have to start from zero. Ten years for nothing. And if I don't sign this now, what then? she asked herself with disdain. *Give up what I've fought for all my life?*

Twenty years in L.A., the tiny art competitions, the battles for commissions, the one goal I had, to finally get a solo show in a reputable London gallery! Yeah, she shrugged, *they do take big commissions from me, but hell, I always said, 'So long as they work as hard as I do" and they had. They sold all the work I gave them and asked for more. So now, to give this all up? No. This is not the time to drop the ball, now that I am finally so close. No way.*

Peg looked down at the document, then signed it.

In her apartment in L.A., Peg scolded herself again, *I should have started over in London! Then I would still have an American passport, and not be in this damn situation now!*

But she knew it hadn't been possible. The bank crash had seen to that. She remembered it vividly, holding her lover as they watched the disaster of that crash on television: well-dressed office staff at Canary Wharf business district, carrying their one box of personal items, heads hanging in disbelief, eyes roaming the calm waters in shock, searching… searching.

Peg had looked on in disbelief but remained naïvely unaware that this too, only a few weeks later, would be her.

That now, the unemployed bankers, with their big bonuses, had only a memory of the life lost to them. And with it, their desire to buy beautiful artwork when wealthy no longer entered their minds.

Peg listened as the gallery owner told her that her work could only be sold at cut rate prices. The art market had fallen seventy percent. No longer able to see a sustainable future, Peg sold all her work for next to nothing. What had not sold, she packed up. It was all too clear that her dream, hard fought for a career, was no longer possible. Neither was her relationship. *In the end, it had split us in two.*

Peg returned to Amsterdam. From there, she first tried the waitressing she'd done years ago in L.A.

She walked into that *ghost town* of empty restaurants: after the bank crash, no one could afford to eat out anymore. She'd spoken to the manager: a tough, angry woman who asked her what work she'd been doing here all these years. "I am, I *was* an artist," she'd replied. The woman scowled at her with all the disgust she could show. *I'd thought, And what? According to you, the musicians that play here are justified in a creative career but I'm not?*

The *ghost town* reminded Peg of the last job she'd worked in Los Angeles, just before moving to Europe.

Like a mining town on the verge of collapse, the whole town had been impacted: The Hollywood studios were refusing to negotiate and in 1988, the Writer's Guild of America had gone on strike.

The city had been hit hard. Not only the actors, who entered the little café she waitressed in, but all the workers of the studios, thousands of people. The effects had rippled out like lava from a volcanic eruption: cab drivers, waiters, bartenders, hotel staff, parking attendants, domestic help, they all felt the pain.

The café where she worked was the place the actors came in for free coffee refills and discussions.

"When will it come to an end?"

"Should we give in?"

She'd heard it over and over, watching as they'd missed working, their love of performing, the anxiety over how else to pay their bills? In the end, they'd won a slight pay increase. *Had it been worth it?* she'd wondered. Peg didn't know, but felt it must have been, for them anyway.

Peg thought, *I never properly mourned the loss of my career.* Whenever she thought of it, she pretended it never happened. *No point to re-open the wounds long healed - well, closed anyway - it only makes me depressed.* With those tough words to herself, she went to the couch and, collapsing on it, let herself have a good cry.

The Search

Ana's mama, a young looking sixty-five-year-old, came in from the kitchen. Her long gray hair carelessly piled up onto her head, held in place with a tortoise shell clip. Her garment was in a brightly colored Guadeloupian mumu dress; it's loose fit keeping her cool and comfortable in the day's heat. The day was a cloudless blue sky, the sun strong on this noonday. She came towards her, arms outstretched for an embrace.

Ana leaned in to hug her. "What, no smile, chica?" she said, and held her with outstretched arms at a distance, looking into her eyes. She said, "What is it? There is something."

"Nothing, Mama," Ana said, her eyes looking away.

Mama said, "No, you come sit down," as she pulled Ana's limp body to the couch, then said, "Now, you tell me, what is it?"

Ana said, "No, Mama, I don't want to," as her face crumpled like a can crushed under a car and tears began to fill her eyes. Then Ana, feeling very young said, "I met a girl."

"A *girl?*" Then her face lit up and she smiled. She said, "What girl? Tell me about her, chica."

Ana sighed and told her, "Her name is Peg."

Mama, now impatient said, "Peg, yes, go on."

Ana straightened her back and told her everything, except the sexual parts. Her mama was open-minded but they'd never shared stories of personal intimacy.

When she finished, her mama said, "This is reason to be happy, no?"

Ana had never ceased to be amazed at her mama's acceptance of her being lesbian.

Ana said, "No."

"No? Why no?" her mama said, "She do something to you? She cheat on you?"

Ana laughed out loud, then said, "No, not the way you mean and she's not married or straight either."

"So? She sounds very nice. This is reason for joy, why are you are so blue?"

Then Ana told her about Peg living in Europe.

Mama said, "Well, she come back, no?"

"No," Ana said.

Mama said, "But she live here, yes?"

Ana then told her the whole story, including the reasons she could not stay, ending with, "Peg gave up her U.S. citizenship."

Mama replied, "What you mean, 'gave up', how can she gave up? She was born here you said."

"Yes, but she gave it up," Ana told her, now angry and pacing the floor. She added, "When I think of you, of our people trying so hard to come here, climbing over mountains, staying nights alone in the blackness of the desert, running across six-lane freeways! And she just hands it over, like… like it was nothing!"

Mama rose and walked into the kitchen, returning with two glasses and a bottle of wine from their family winery in Fresno. She poured and said, "You and I need a drink. Here, taste this." They clinked their glasses and sipped in silence. Then her mama said, "You love her, don't you? Yes, I can see in your eyes that you do. Well, then you must find a way together."

Peg walked into the Bar Amour. She thought, *only two nights ago I was so excited to meet Ana, leaving with her, driving in her Tattooed Chica, like I was a free bird soaring. Life has a strange sense of humor sometimes…*

Jamie watched Peg walk in and was jolted by her friend's low energy without her usual perky hello. Peg walked over to the empty bar and sat down.

Jamie said, "Hi. Want a drink? I've not seen you for a while, it didn't go well, huh?"

Peg replied, "I'll have a beer, and no, actually, it went *great*."

Pouring the beer, Jamie said, "Wonderful! So why the long face?" as she put the beer in front of her.

Peg said, "Because I had to tell her, you know, *the talk*, about having to leave."

"Ahh," Jamie said, then, "it's really serious, so fast? Yeah, I saw as you left on Friday that you were a new woman, not that the other one *was so bad*," as Jamie raised her eyebrows up and down, Groucho Marx-style.

Peg laughed without humor, then said, "But at least then, I wasn't in love - *with an American* for damn sake," laughing again at the irony.

Jamie said, "Is there anything I can do? You know, if I wasn't already married to Amy, I'd propose to you in a New York minute. But, strange as it may sound, she probably wouldn't understand."

Peg laughed at Jamie's kind words, grateful for such a true friend. Then she said, "Thank you for the offer, kind lady, but I'll just have to keep myself busy, as usual, and forget this weekend… it's gonna be hard though."

"Well," said Jamie, "I can help you there. I'm short-staffed. Do you think you can remember how to bar back? Only if you want to, I mean. For a few hours 'til I get set up."

"Sure," Peg replied, "it'll do me good."

Ana sat with her mama, talking about other things, but always veering back to Peg.

Mama finally said, "Well, chica," wiping Ana's tears from her eyes with the handkerchief she always kept up her sleeve, she said, "I see no problem. I have solution for you."

Ana perked up and looked at her as she continued, "You girls, you have that marriage now for girls, yes?"

Ana laughed and said, "Gay marriage, Mama, yes, we have that now."

Her mama replied, "What is this, gay marriage, *pah!* It is marriage, plain and simple. Now," settling into the idea as a new fun event, she continued, "we'll invite your brother and nieces from San Francisco and the Palos, from next door…"

"Ho, Mama, wait up," Ana replied, "I haven't even asked her yet, and…"

"And what?" her mama said, "You love her or not?"

"Yes," Ana said, realizing she wanted Peg more than anything she'd ever wanted, to be with her and share a life *together*.

Mama replied, "So, must I do everything? Go buy a ring. No, wait," She left the room for a minute, returning with something in her hand. "This was your grandmother's ring."

Ana picked up the ring gently with her fingers. It was intricately woven with vines of roses, twisting to form a gold ring with a small diamond set on top, like the crown on the head of a princess.

Ana felt so many emotions, she couldn't speak.

Her mama said, "Now, must I do everything? Go now, ask her and here, take the ring, take it for… your wife."

Ana said simply, "Thank you, Mama, for this, for… just being… you,"

She looked into her daughter's eyes, the dark pools she'd fallen in love with forty-five years ago and kissed her, pushing her out the door.

Ana drove like the wind, the tiny ring inside her front pocket. She hummed to the Latin song on her radio, swerving through traffic like a pro. She pulled up at Peg's apartment, skidding to a stop. Hopping over the seat, she ran toward the building that she'd never even been inside. She remembered the number though and stepped through the black wrought-iron gate.

The courtyard had a small, blue swimming pool. Surrounding it were white patio chairs and lounges. At one end was a round glass table with four chairs and an open white umbrella shading them from the sun. The back wall was white, mandevilla flowers twisting on vines, climbing the trellises.

To the left were two staircases, going up to the one floor high apartments upstairs. Peg's number was 20, on the ground floor, at the left. Ana walked toward it, disappointed to see a white curtain over the front window. She timidly rapped on the door. No answer. She tried again, but no one came. She walked away, her head hung low.

Ana drove through the neighborhood, slowing at yard sales. Peg told her, that was one of her favorite things to do on a Sunday, shopping for vintage stuff at yard sales. No Peg. For blocks, she drove, slowing at each blonde-haired woman, none of them Peg. Finally, she drove to the Bar Amour, pulling up in front.

Jamie polished the bar top, getting everything ready for her busiest day. After 1 p.m., the women would straggle in, having just finished brunch. Or to soothe a hangover with a Bloody Mary, shaking out the cobwebs from last night and get their juices flowing.

Then Shawne, the D.J., would come in and play chill-out tunes until about 6 p.m., then dance music until 2 a.m.

Overall, it was always a great crowd, very mixed with different cultures and ages. Surprisingly, gals in their twenties mixed easily with over fifty-year-olds. The reason, Jamie thought, was there are so few women's bars in Los Angeles anymore. Men's bars had always done well, but women paid less so the bar made less money. They didn't spend so freely anymore.

Jamie had worked in gay bars for twenty-five years, remembered the women coming in from out of town, or from other countries. The women stopping in to see what there was to do here, or to exchange information about politics or gay rights. The years of gay pride, the march going right past here. The laughter and dancing. She now thought, *Yes, sadly, it's the end of an era...*

Just then, a woman came through the door. Surprisingly, she saw that it was the gal who'd left on Friday night with Peg. *Hmmm*, thought Jamie, *I wonder if she'll tell me her name today.*

Ana walked into the empty bar. They were not yet officially open. The early crowd, she knew, were just finishing brunch, and would straggle in later.

Ana saw Jamie behind the bar and went up to her and said, "Hi," as she slid onto a stool.

Jamie said, "Hi… what can I get you?" Jamie was feeling a little strict with her, having just heard about her shitty reaction to Peg's dilemma. Jamie was feeling very protective of her friend; she was going find out what, if anything, was this woman's intention with her best friend.

Ana said, "Hi" again, then, "I didn't introduce myself to you on Friday. I'm sorry. I'm Ana."

Jamie said, "Hello again, Ana, I'm Jamie," then "want a Budweiser?"

Ana said, "Ha! You remembered! Yes, thanks."

Jamie poured the beer and said, "Yeah, I always remember what they order, but rarely their names… or anything else."

Ana said, "I bet you know a lot though, being bartender… hearing all the gossip, stuff like that."

Jamie sensed Ana was attempting to pump her, for what she wasn't sure, and said, "Well, some gossip is fun… not about friends though."

Ana blushed and said, "Okay, you caught me. You are a good friend of Peg, I saw that."

"Very good," Jamie said.

Ana tried again, "Look, I, we, Peg and I had a… a sort of fight, not fight, not an argument really, but a… a disagreement. I just want to know, do you know where she is? Have you seen her? I've looked all over."

Just then, Peg entered, back first, from a side door, carrying a crate of beer. She bent down and then rose up to see Ana. Shock left both of their faces thunderstruck.

"Peg!" Ana cried, so overwhelmed at the sight of her, she thought she may faint. Then said, "I… I looked for you everywhere."

Peg, her body stiff in a self-protective stance, replied standoffishly, "Oh? I've been here for more than an hour."

Jamie stood on the sidelines, arms folded, to see what was going to happen, not even pretending to work.

Ana reached out her hand to Peg, who timidly held up her hand. Ana clutched it as a drowning passenger grasps a life raft.

Peg felt the cool texture of Ana's hand, its warmth flowing through her as the tide laps the shore. Despite her false bravado, she was quickly softening. She waited, looking into her dark eyes.

Ana's words, like a volcano kept too long in the earth, spewed like an eruption and poured out. She said, "Babe, *I'm so sorry*, I was wrong… I was just being stupid and scared to lose you, and then I almost did! Or… did I?"

Peg said, "I, oh, Ana, what more is there to say? Maybe we can enjoy the few days we have though, before I leave, okay?"

Ana smiled and pulled her around the bar, holding her close for a very long time.

Jamie continued to watch, by now ignoring the few customers that had straggled in and were trying to get her attention. Her own instincts told her there was still more to come. The women at the end of the bar sensed something unusual going on as well and stopped calling to her. Shushing each other, they began to watch.

Ana took Peg's hand in hers, turning the palm up and kissing it. Peg felt the texture of Ana's hand, the softness of her lips as she kissed her open palm. Still holding it, Ana pulled something out from inside her pocket, looked into her eyes and said, "Peg, if you'll have me, I want so very much… to marry you," and she slid her grandmother's ring onto her finger.

Chantz Perkins has worked as an artist in many forms: painter, sculptor, photographer, videographer and writer. Her work has been commissioned and exhibited in Britain, Europe, and the United Stated. She hosts a blog, website, and web shop, where museum quality prints of her work can be purchased.

More information can be found here: http://artbychantz.com.

Other books and novelettes by Chantz Perkins:
Puertas: One Woman's Journey Through to The Other Side
Alex and Cleo
House of Cheng
Gold Ring
Tattooed Chica

www.ingramcontent.com/pod-product-compliance
Lightning Source LLC
LaVergne TN
LVHW061630070526
838199LV00071B/6630